# VIKING'S DESIRE

CALLED BY A VIKING
BOOK ONE

MARIAH STONE

This is a work of fiction. Names, characters, places, and incidents either are the products of the author's imagination or are used fictitiously. Any resemblance to actual persons, living or dead, businesses, companies, events, or locales is entirely coincidental.



Cover design by Qamber Designs and Media

# GET A FREE MARIAH STONE BOOK!

Join Mariah's mailing list to be the first to know of new releases, free books, special prices, and other author giveaways.

freehistoricalromancebooks.com

# Also by Mariah Stone

## Mariah's Time Travel Romance Series

- Called by a Highlander
- Called by a Viking
- Called by a Pirate
- Fated

## Mariah's Regency Romance Series

- Dukes and Secrets

## View All of Mariah's Books in Reading Order

Scan the QR code for the complete list of Mariah's ebooks, paperbacks, and audiobooks in reading order.

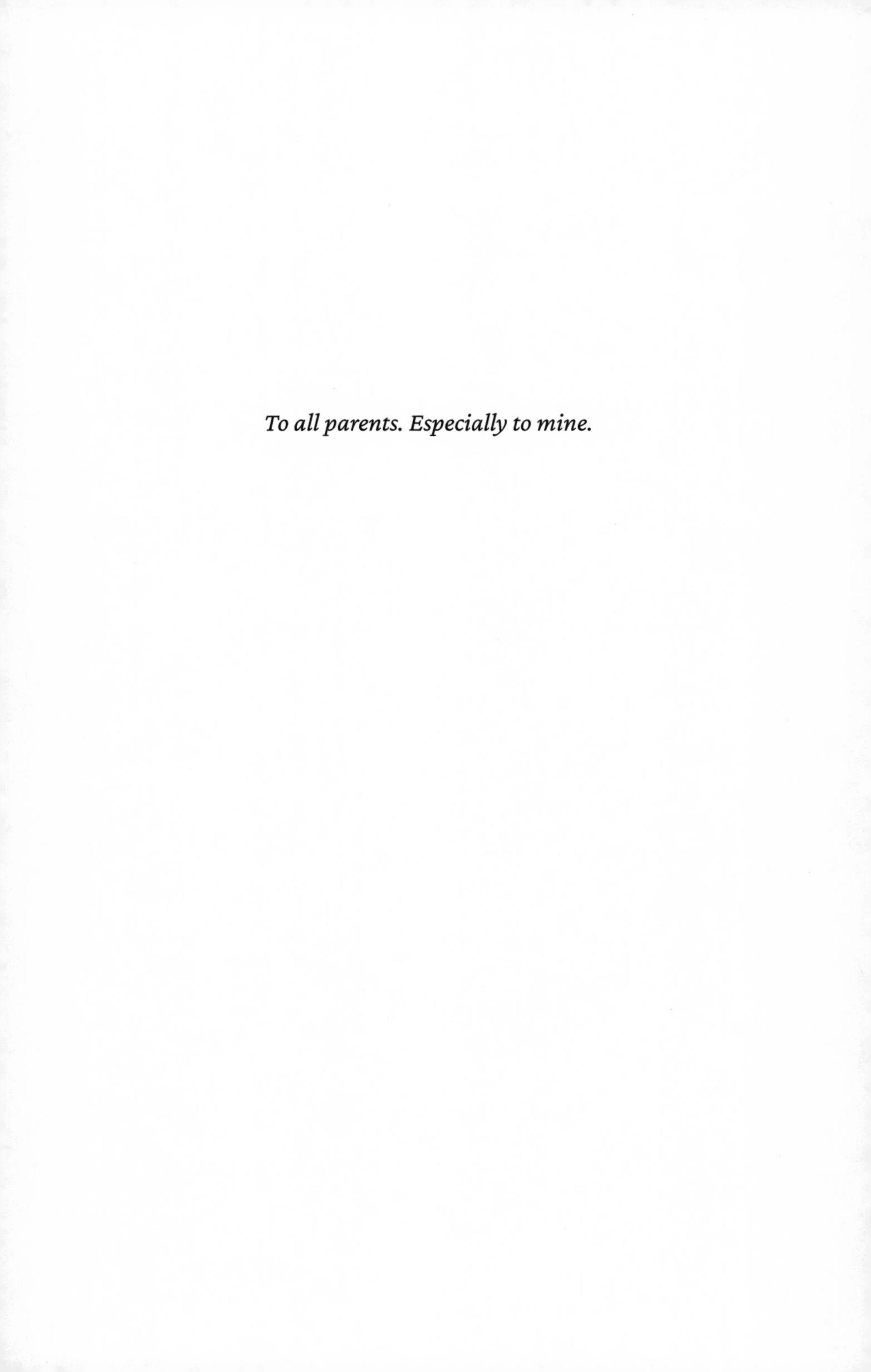

*To all parents. Especially to mine.*

# PROLOGUE

Ålesund, Møre Province, Norway, April 880 AD

"Do not let me down, Einar," King Harald said. "The Orkneys must be free of Viking outlaws. My word must rule there, not chaos."

If Einar Birgirsson could, he would crush the king, who had taken away his home during his conquest of Norway.

Instead, Einar walked by the king's side towards the jetty. There, three longships pierced the gray sky, their bellies being filled with sacks, chests, sheep, and people. Next to Einar walked his ten-winter-old daughter, Svanhild, and his older brother, Jarl Rögnvald of Møre.

Einar held the king's piercing blue gaze. Even though Harald had less physical power than Einar, the man had the political might to ruin Einar's life and that of his family.

"The Orkneys will be free, Lord," Einar said.

Harald nodded, satisfied. "Good. I have faith in you. Your

nephew refused the task, claiming it was impossible to get rid of them. But I respect that you are up for the challenge."

Rögnvald's neck reddened at the mention of his son's failure, and a tinge of shame stung Einar as well. Einar clenched his fists. He would restore the family's honor.

Had he a son, he would not let him hide in the village. He would make him answer to the king.

Another reason to be glad that he did not have more children.

Ålesund was a good location on the arm of the North Sea, with easy access for sea voyages. From behind, it was protected by looming mountains with flat tops and forested slopes. Einar would miss their magnificence and the lush, wet smell of a forest after the rain. The Orkney Islands were bare and low compared to Norway, but the scent of the sea and the chill of the wind would likely be the same.

"Einar will please you, Lord." Rögnvald was a little stouter and shorter than Einar, and already silver ran through the dull gold of his hair. "Viking season is about to begin, so it will be the right time to cut the outlaws off before they start raiding. Also, it is a good time to sow, and lambing is underway. This will give a new settlement a proper start in preparation for the first winter."

He was right. Ålesund was in full swing of pre-sowing activities, the air filled with distant cries of working men and women. Soon, the Orkneys would be, too.

They arrived at the jetty where Einar's men loaded the last sacks and barrels onto the ships. Waves splashed gently against the wooden hulls. Once Einar and Svanhild boarded, the ships would set off.

King Harald nodded without taking his eyes off Einar. "I hope we can put our previous disagreement behind us, Einar. I have no wish to be your enemy. Not a man like you."

Einar's throat tightened. What do you say to a king who took your home and is now offering a new one? Even though this home was swarming with dangerous men who were ready to rob and kill.

You say what needs to be said. "I do not wish to be your enemy, either." He glanced at Rögnvald. "I just wish my daughter could stay here, in safety. Outlaw-infested islands are no place for a young girl."

Svanhild's eyes, as wide as armrings, landed on him. "Father, please, take me with you."

Einar's chest tightened. Moments like these were when he most needed and missed his wife. He closed his eyes for a moment, gathering his thoughts. She would know what to say. Her hazel eyes would sparkle as she smiled and sank to her knees to talk to Svanhild. Her golden-red hair, like amber when the sun danced over it, would sway and shine.

But when he opened his eyes, only his daughter stood there, the living image of his great love, the wife he'd always miss.

Svanhild was still looking at him, petting the smoke-gray kitten in her arms. She had told him every new home needed a cat to keep mice away.

Einar needed to distract himself from the pain that grasped his chest—the love and fear for his daughter. He took a sack and threw it to one of the men on the ship. "Svanhild, I only think of your safety."

"But will I not be safe with you?" she asked.

Einar leaned down and picked up another sack. "Enemies do not hide behind every corner in Ålesund. Your uncle and his sons will protect you."

Rögnvald nodded. "Your father is right, sweet. You know your cousins will be joyful if you stay, as will I. Einar, you should send for her after you have cleared the islands."

King Harald frowned. "But that might take years. Will you not miss your only child?"

Einar's shoulders tensed like they did every time he was supposed to show any affection towards his daughter.

He threw the sack to his man on the ship. "Her being alive is more imp—"

"If she is with you," Harald interrupted, "you will be more focused on making the islands safe."

Einar clenched his teeth so hard, his jaw hurt.

"And putting down roots will only make you feel more at home," King Harald continued. "Is that not what you want, Einar? Living in your own home after being your brother's guest for many winters? Is it not time for you to get back to being a leader? To building a dowry for Svanhild?"

Einar put his hands on his hips, helplessness weakening his muscles, anger burning his gut. Oh, he was sly, this king. Sly, smart, and manipulative. Loki was his god, no doubt. Einar picked up a barrel of mead that the king had given him. The thing weighed as much as Svanhild had when she was two—the last time he'd held her in his arms.

"Yes, Lord," Einar said, "That is why I go. For her."

He threw the barrel to the man, who barely caught it. Einar breathed out. It was good to do something with his body, and the tightness and the burning muscles were a relief.

King Harald nodded. "Good. I know a widower of your age must want for more children, too. A new home, a new start. Why not a new wife, Einar?"

The blood left Einar's face. He must have turned the color of cotton grass because both King Harald and Rögnvald frowned at him.

"No wives, Lord." Einar wiped his forehead—surely from the strain of physical activity, not from hearing the word "wife."

"There will be no one else for me," he said.

"Nonsense." King Harald waved his hand. "You need a woman who will make the Orkneys your true home."

Einar shook his head. "No."

Harald's expression shifted from concern to something resembling anger. "You must find a wife and marry this year."

Einar suppressed a growl of fury. How dare this man decide his private life?

"Yes, in fact, this is my final condition," Harald said. "If you want to be the jarl and to own the Orkney and Shetland Islands, and if you want a good dowry for Svanhild, you need to be wed in two moons."

The wooden jetty must have shifted under Einar's feet. He stood like an oaf, blinking and slack-jawed.

"You are jesting, King, surely," Einar mumbled.

"I am serious." He turned and waved someone over. A skald approached, the young man who had recited beautiful poetry of Harald's victories during last night's feast. The skald's eyes burned with curiosity.

"Solver Tykirsson." Harald clapped the man's shoulder. "You will go with Einar to the Orkneys and be my envoy. You will see if the wedding goes through in two moons and report to me."

Solver beamed at Einar and Svanhild. "Yes, Lord. I will be happy to entertain the settlers and lift their spirits. I will commemorate the settling of the Orkneys and Shetlands by the Norwegian jarl Einar Birgirsson."

Einar listened with an open mouth, still not believing what he was hearing. The king dared to send a watchdog to make sure Einar married in two moons. Hot fury began rolling through his veins.

"You cannot be serious, Lord," he rumbled. "I am not your son. I am not your brother. Or your—"

"You are my subject," Harald said, his eyes dead cold. "And you will do as you are told, or you can forget the Orkneys."

"Lord—"

"That is my final word, Einar. I need a stable annex of Norway, an excellent strategic point for trading and raiding expeditions. Fertile land that can feed you and many more generations of Norsemen. A family is key to all that. So marry in two moons or forever lose a chance to have your own home."

Anger roared within Einar.

"The last thing I need is a wife," he said.

"I think it is the first thing you need, brother," Rögnvald said quietly.

Einar shot a furious glance at him, but Rögnvald only shrugged one giant shoulder. Einar looked at Svanhild, who cuddled the kitten and met his eyes with no protest. Did she want a new mother?

Pain stabbed Einar in the gut as he remembered holding the feverish, dying Agdis in his arms. After four days of labor, their second child had died inside of her, and she had been pale, in pain and bleeding.

He could not go through that again. He had one child. That was good enough.

But he needed to run the new settlement and build a dowry for his daughter, and this was the only option available.

Fine, he would agree to Harald's proposal, but only on his own terms. His chest was so heavy that he felt as though massive chains cuffed his ribs.

"Let it be so," Einar said.

King Harald flashed a broad smile and clapped Einar's back. "Good. Wise decision. Two moons' time. Odin bless you on your journey."

He stepped back and watched Einar impassively.

The king's job was done. He had just ruled Einar's destiny, and Einar had walked straight into the trap.

So be it. If the Norns wove another wife into his future, Einar would accept it.

But nothing would make him open his heart to her or have any more children with her.

Because, as he'd learned so painfully in his life, loving someone would only end in pain.

# CHAPTER ONE

Orlando, Florida, May 3, 2019

"Holly, sweetheart, are you sure it's the wisest thing to go to Scotland two weeks before your big merger? You've been working so hard."

Holly clenched the handle of her suitcase harder as she walked through the departure area with her parents to drop off her luggage. Mom's brown eyes were worried—as always. The lines around her mouth deepened.

"Mom, really, everything is done. We're just waiting for the final paperwork to come through. In two weeks, we sign. I'll be back by then."

"A responsible person wouldn't leave right before closing an important deal," her mother said. "This is not how I raised you."

Holly suppressed a sigh and stood at the end of the baggage drop line. Mom meant well. It was just hard to see that sometimes behind the criticizing comments. Holly turned and faced her parents. They were so different from her—her mom, a petite, sweet-looking woman with a mane of curly gray hair; her dad, tall, handsome, and broad-shouldered; a true army man.

Of course, Holly didn't look like either of them.

"Mom, I haven't taken a vacation in three years. The genealogy researcher in Inverness has a very long waiting list, and her next opening is in two years. It's a rare chance to find out about my roots."

"But why do you need to find out about *them* when you have us?" Mom said. "Haven't we given you everything?"

Dad hugged her. "Gemma, let her do it. You don't know what it's like..."

Holly flashed a grateful smile at her dad. He was a man of few words, but when he said them, they were the right ones. Holly was more like him than her mom, who had a lot to say on many subjects.

The line moved and Holly went to check in her luggage and get her boarding pass. Once she was done, she returned to her parents.

"Should we go for a coffee?" Mom asked.

Holly flashed a polite smile. "Mom, I better get going. I still need to send a couple of emails before the flight."

Her mom sighed. "I suppose."

The three of them proceeded towards the security check.

"I just keep thinking I forgot to tell you something," Mom said. "I have this uneasiness in my heart about your trip. As if I'm seeing you for the last t—"

She cut herself off, tears gathering in her eyes. Holly squeezed her mom's shoulder.

"Everything will be fine, Mom."

Holly's dad hugged her mom. "Gemma, she's traveled the

world. It's Scotland, not Siberia. And she's a grown, successful woman."

Mom cocked her head. "A successful woman doesn't date a sperm bank."

*Here we go.*

"This is why you wanted to go for a coffee, Mom? To berate me about my wish to have children?"

"It's unnatural, honey. You need a husband first."

"And what if I don't have one, huh, Mom? What if men literally run in the other direction after they get to know the real me? Should that stop me? Nowadays, a woman doesn't need a man to raise—"

"Those men are idiots. And yes, a woman does need a partner to raise a child. How many times have you tried? Five? Six?"

Holly's eyes watered. Why was it that people closest to her had the capacity to hurt her the most?

"Last month was seven," Holly said. "You're right. It's probably not meant to be. Something must be wrong with me."

Mom grimaced and hugged Holly with one arm. "I know very well how it is, dear. God never gave me the chance to give birth, but he gave me you. In preparation for when the right man comes, maybe you need to try eating healthier or cut out coffee. You know I raised you to achieve things despite your flaws."

"I guess this flaw is too big to be overcome," Holly said, wiping her eyes and leaving black smudges of mascara on the backs of her hands and undoubtedly on her face.

From the corner of Holly's eye, she saw a flash of movement. She glanced to her left and noticed a big tall man with a cart full of suitcases marching towards them at full speed. He was looking at his phone.

Holly barely managed to jerk her mother out of his path, steadying her to keep her from falling.

"Sir, please watch where you're going," Holly said.

The man glanced over his phone, raised his hand without stopping. "Sorry, sorry, late for my flight." He continued marching, his eyes glued to his phone.

"Thank you, sweetheart," Mom said. "You've always protected me, ever since you were little—even from spiders."

Holly chuckled. Her mom could seem harsh at times, but she was terrified of spiders.

They stopped at the end of the line to the security check, which, thankfully, had only three people waiting.

"Behave well, Holly." Mom straightened Holly's blouse as though before her first day at school. "Don't drink too much whiskey, don't sleep around, and don't forget us."

Holly gasped and shook her head. "Mom, I can't believe you just said that. I do not sleep around!"

"Well, you have no man in your life, and those Highlanders..." She threw a glance at Dad as she trailed off.

"Stop talking to me like I'm a child," Holly said. "I'm thirty-five for God's sake. You didn't even have to bring me to the airport—I have a car!"

"Ah, nonsense. Someone had to make sure you didn't forget your luggage somewhere."

Holly took a deep breath, trying to calm her nerves. She means well, she told herself. She means well. She just doesn't know how to show it.

"Mom, I run a billion-dollar company. I don't tend to forget much."

Mom smiled and cupped her face. "You're right, dear. Please call us when you land."

She hugged Holly. Dad smiled apologetically and hugged

her, too. He kissed the crown of her head and whispered, "We love you, hon."

Holly waved to them and joined the line at the security check, the tension in her shoulders finally releasing. Once she had a few days away from home and her parents, she hoped she would be able to forget that something was clearly wrong with her. She would read the book about medieval Scotland and Vikings and drink as much coffee as she wanted on the plane.

And maybe, just maybe, she'd find out where she really came from and why her real parents had rejected her.

NEAR THE VILLAGE OF TONGUE, Sutherland, Northern Scotland, May 5, 2019

TOGETHER WITH MS. VERDANDI, the genealogy researcher from Inverness, Holly walked towards the edge of the bare green coast that spread to the left and right. At the edge of the cliffs in front of them, in the middle of the green grass, stood a giant ash tree. Holly felt a strange pull towards the tree, as though she needed to touch it. Maybe it was because there were no other trees in sight for miles and miles.

Holly sped up, cautious not to overwhelm the old lady, whose lilac suit was a strange contrast with the wildness of the sight. But she didn't need to worry. Ms. Verdandi looked eighty but seemed to have more agility and strength than Holly.

Behind the tree and the cliffs was the North Sea, dark blue now in the sunlight. A breeze brought the scents of sea, sun, and warm rocks, and Holly inhaled it deeply, a smile spreading on her face. The air here was very different from Orlando. It felt cool and fresh, and even the scent felt *green*. It was the scent of freedom.

"So, this is where it happened?" Holly said when they stood by the tree. "Vikings kidnapped my great-great-great..." Holly laughed. "I don't even know how many 'greats' I need to add to 'grandmother.'"

Ms. Verdandi echoed her laugh.

"Yes, they did," she said in her strange accent that was definitely not Scottish. "Northern Scotland has always had a deep connection with the Vikings." Her eyes twinkled mischievously.

"Near the ash tree, there was a big village that went from here down to the beach."

Ms. Verdandi gestured to the left, where the green surface of the cliff descended to a small, secluded white-sand beach.

"Later, Clan MacKay would rule here. Your ancestor who was kidnapped, she would be a MacKay. You have both Scottish and Norse blood, dear," she said.

Holly raised her brows. "Well, yes, that's what the DNA ancestry test said."

The woman smiled. "I did not need a DNA test to tell you that. Norse heritage is written all over you. That steel in your eyes. The strength. The honesty. The honor. The endurance and commitment you have to protect your loved ones no matter what."

A small shiver ran through Holly's skin. The words rang true and reverberated within her deeply. "You can tell all of that by just looking at me?"

The edges of the woman's eyes creased in many small wrinkles. "You just need to know where to look. I also see that you have magic in your blood. You have quite a few *völvas* and witches in your line."

Holly laughed. "Right. And the sky turned red and there

were dragons breathing fire. Oh, you do not seriously believe that, do you?"

The woman arched one eyebrow and said, "Look at the tree. What do you see?"

Holly studied the tree. It was massive, tall, and thick, with big roots gripping the rocky soil. How had it even managed to grow on these cliffs? Bare branches rustled in the wind.

Bare tree. Bare land. Barren like Holly.

Tears pricked her eyes. God, why was it so important to her? She didn't even have a man in her life.

But she'd always wanted a child of her own. Flesh and blood. Although she loved her parents, maybe that feeling of being broken, being faulty, was because she had been rejected by her biological mother.

She looked at the trunk and frowned. Something was carved on it—an intricate, ornate, interwoven pattern. Something Celtic or Viking. How had she not noticed this before? Holly looked closer. Something long and sharp at the edges.

A spindle.

Holly glanced for a moment at Ms. Verdandi, puzzled. "What does it mean?"

"Just look," she said, a sly smile spreading her lips.

Holly looked again and gasped. Instead of the wooden spindle on the trunk, it was golden, and the patterns weren't carved anymore but engraved. She stepped closer and brushed her index finger along the length of the spindle. It was smooth, and it buzzed slightly. Holly pulled her hand away.

"Neat trick," she said with a nervous laugh. "How did you do it?"

"Ah, you'll learn. You were looking for a tree, dear? You found it."

"I wasn't looking for a tree. I was looking for information about my ancestors."

"A genealogical tree, dear."

Holly smiled. "Ah. Well, yes. If you put it that way."

"Your roots lie with the Vikings...but also your future."

"Excuse me?"

"Look at the spindle, Holly." As if hypnotized, Holly looked. "There's a man who needs you back in the ninth century. He will help you find answers to all your questions, and his love will heal the cracks in your heart."

The spindle began to move towards the surface of the tree, as though pushed from within the trunk. Holly gasped, and as the spindle popped out of the surface completely, she automatically reached out her hand to catch the falling object.

The old lady's words reverberated through her whole body: "There is a man who needs you back in the ninth century. Your roots lie with the Vikings...but also your future."

Something invisible grabbed Holly's hand and pulled, something warm and hard and woody. Holly screamed and began struggling as she was pulled into the tree. She dug her heels into the ground, but the force was too strong. Then the trunk closed around her.

And darkness enveloped her.

Daylight blinded her as she was thrown forward with a violent jerk, as though someone had pushed her from behind. She fell to the ground, scratching the skin of her palms.

Screams rang in the air. The acrid smell of smoke filled her nostrils. Fear kicked her in the stomach. Adrenaline gathered her nerves like hair and pulled at them. She was still on what looked like the same Scottish coast and cliffs, except there was no Ms. Verdandi and no tree. About ten feet from her stood round stone houses with thatched cone-shaped roofs—and they were burning. Behind them, there was a medieval village on the green slope of the cliff leading towards the white-sand beach.

And among the houses, people dressed in medieval clothes fought. Some had axes and even swords, others only sticks and pitchforks.

But they not only fought, they also killed. They hauled people towards the beach. Down there, men carried sacks, furs, and even people towards three ships that looked Viking.

What the hell was this? The old woman had said Holly would travel to the ninth century.

The ninth century?!

But Holly could not actually travel in time, could she? This was ridiculous. This must be some hallucination or trick, or a prank. Maybe some sort of movie set.

But the air was thick with the iron tang of blood, and the weapons were metal, not plastic or rubber, because they cut flesh and spilled blood. There were no cameras, no directors, and no one telling the actors to run or stab or do any of that.

Holly's throat clenched, and she jumped to her feet, obeying the instinct to run and hide.

Frantically, she searched for an escape, for some way—

A man with a bloody ax and a predatory look stared right at her. The ground sank under her feet. He was tall and broad, his shoulders like boulders.

As he walked towards her, a single braid that came from the middle of his shaven head swung. His beard couldn't hide a sly smile.

Holly turned and ran. Away from the village, back towards the small packed-dirt road where Ms. Verdandi had parked the car. If only she could get to the car...

She ran and ran, wind whistling in her ears, but he was closing in on her. And the road was nowhere to be seen. Nor was the car.

He grabbed her, and she stumbled and fell. Then he got on top of her. The impact kicked the air out of her. Pain radiated from the center of her stomach, and she choked under his weight. He turned her to face him, his pale-blue eyes piercing her. The ornate dragon tattoos on his shaven skull glistened in the dull light.

"And who do we have here?" he whispered, putting the bloody handle of his ax to her throat. His beard tickled her chin. "A witch. Are you a völva? I saw you appear out of thin air. Tell me."

She finally gasped in a breath. He was speaking some foreign language, her mind registered distantly. Holly had only learned Spanish in high school, and this was not Spanish. How was it possible that she understood him?

"No matter. You shall tell me on the way to the Orkneys."

He stood and picked her up as though she didn't weigh anything, putting her over his shoulder.

"Let me go!" Holly yelled. She kicked and drummed her fists against his back. But it was as though the giant didn't feel a thing. He just spanked her on her behind, so hard her whole body hurt.

"Shut up, witch. I thought Odin had forgotten Thorir Tree-beard, but he sent me a witch. Odin loves men who dare destiny. And what better way to do that than sacrifice a völva to the one-eyed god?"

# CHAPTER TWO

North Ronaldsay, Orkney Islands, May 7, 880 AD

"There they are." Einar crouched behind a boulder.

Thorir Treebeard's camp was a gathering of tents and campfires on the bare landscape of the island. With no trees around, the heavy rain drumming against the grass and the tents was as good a cover as they'd get.

"Lofarr did well spotting the camp," he told Solver, who was crouching beside him. "I should have gotten him last sennight. Now he has five ships."

"You fought well when we chased them away," Solver said cheerfully. "It is not going to be an easy task. This is why the king chose you."

Behind them, all fifty of Einar's men waited, rain dripping from their beards, their armor and weapons glistening.

"You should not have come, Solver," Einar said. "I cannot watch your back in a skirmish. Stay back in one of the ships."

Despite being a skald, Solver had a better sword than

Einar's. No doubt a gift from Harald.

"You do not need to worry about me, Einar," Solver said. "I must observe the battle to commemorate it in a poem. For your grandchildren and great-grandchildren to listen to before they go to sleep."

Einar shook his head. "Watch then."

He gave a signal, and his men advanced, staying low. The outlaws probably outnumbered his men, but Einar hoped he had the element of surprise.

It was clear that the camp was in a victorious post-raid sleepiness. Men were drunk and tired. They'd eaten, had their women, and had just satisfied their hunger for violence. They were probably all sleeping or passed out from mead.

There was one sentinel sitting by the campfire with his head low. An empty cup hung from his hand, rainwater dripping from the edge of it. Einar gave a silent signal, and one of his men cut the sentinel's throat without a sound. The camp was full of snoring and the quiet buzz of voices under the drumming rain.

Einar gestured, and the men spread through the camp to the tents. On Einar's signal, they would cry out to give the outlaws a warning and allow them to grab their weapons and meet their deaths like warriors.

Einar believed every man deserved a chance, even an outlaw; although, few people shared his opinion.

Outlaws didn't just raid. A common farmer went raiding from time to time to make his fortune. Outlaws had done something so dishonorable—like backstabbing, murdering their jarl, or raping someone's wife or daughter—that they could not be members of civilized society.

A lawful man had the right to kill an outlaw on sight. A slave's death would need to be repaid. But an outlaw was nothing.

Einar froze, listening outside the biggest tent, which must belong to Thorir.

"How did you just appear out of thin air like that?" a man said from within. "I need to know. Please, before you die, you must tell me."

"I told you I have no powers," said a woman. "I'm not a witch. You are wasting your precious sacrifice on a regular woman. Just let me go."

Einar frowned. A witch? A sacrifice? Was Thorir so out of his mind that he was planning to sacrifice a völva? He quickly nodded to Lofarr, who passed by him with ten men to surround the tents farther away.

Thorir continued, "Do you want me to send you to Odin with your beautiful face carved in runes? I'll get the answer from you."

He wanted to torture her, that Loki's son.

"Oh my God, Thorir, or whoever you are. If you touch a hair on my head, you'll be missing at least one ball."

He respected the woman—she was not about to give in easily.

"Did Odin send you?" Thorir asked. "Einar, who chased us away from the Mainland last week. They say he is a direct descendant of Odin, fifty generations down. But I do not believe he is the only one. King Harald commanded Einar to come here. I, on the other hand, do not report to kings. I am free. I create freedom for my men. I want the only law on these islands to be my word. If that does not make me a descendant of gods, I do not know what does."

Einar's back prickled from cold sweat. Having heard this, he realized how dangerous and insane Thorir was in his speech and motivations. His men's boots slumped gently across the wet grass of the camp as a dozen more moved to the tents to his left.

"It is a pity to kill such a woman. I am tempted to just keep you for myself as my bed slave."

"Ha! That is *not* going to happen. I'd rather sacrifice myself to Odin," the woman said.

A loud slap split the air, and the woman cried in pain. Almost immediately, something heavy and wooden crashed. The last of his men took positions around the tents on the other side of the camp. They were ready.

"Shut up! You are my way to Valhalla!" Thorir shouted.

Rage and worry for the brave woman rose in Einar like a geyser.

"To Odin!" He roared and raised his ax high in the air.

"To Odin!" his men echoed, crashing into the tents. Einar ducked through the entrance. But before he could see what was happening, someone hit him on the side of his head, and he swayed. Thorir's shadow came at him again, but Einar was ready and deflected the blow with the handle of his ax.

It was almost dark here in the tent, with the only light coming through the oiled linen of the walls. Einar saw from the corner of his eye that the silhouette of what looked like a tall, slender boy lay beside the furs. It must be the woman, Einar realized.

Thorir's face flashed before him, teeth bared. He attacked Einar with a broken-off leg of a chair, and Einar deflected him. Thorir made a movement to kick Einar in the gut, but Einar evaded him and slammed the handle of his ax into Thorir's chin instead. Thorir swayed back and staggered, but came at Einar again. Einar roared and swung his ax at Thorir's head, but the man stepped aside.

The woman moaned, and Einar turned to her, afraid someone else was hurting her, but Thorir used Einar's distraction to shove him hard in his solar plexus and disappear from the tent.

Einar gasped, pain radiating from his stomach, and sat, choking, waiting until he could breathe again.

The woman stared at him with wide eyes, one side of her head bleeding.

Einar raised his hand as though signaling her to wait. As soon as he could take a breath, he stormed out of the tent, hoping to catch Thorir. His men were chasing Thorir's men as they ran towards their ships. The wounded and dead lay on the ground around the camp. Most of them were the outlaws. Slaves shook while Solver cut the ropes around their wrists, and some of his men herded sheep towards the camp. Einar ran after the fugitives, but most of those who were still alive had already made it to a ship. There were about twenty of them now, enough to man only one ship out of five. The fight was over, and Einar was victorious, but Thorir had escaped again.

Which meant he would recuperate, probably campaign through the smaller islands, and gather a stronger group.

Based on what Einar had heard, Thorir would not give up.

Neither would Einar.

Spotting Solver, he said, "Can you make sure the slaves know they are free and may come with us to Mainland or find their own way back home? We will take all of the sheep and everything else of value. We should also take the rest of Thorir's ships, those that are in a good condition, anyway."

"Good decision, Einar. I regret I missed your fight with Thorir."

"There was nothing to miss. As you can see, he escaped. There is a witch, however, who is still in the tent. I shall go and see to her."

Solver's eyes rounded. "A völva?"

Einar shrugged and walked.

Solver followed him and went into the tent first, probably too curious to wait.

Einar heard a loud *thud* from within, a moan, and something heavy falling on the ground. Carefully, he entered the tent, and before the leg of the chair found his head, he grabbed the woman and held her around her waist, trapping her arms behind her.

"Let me go!" she yelled. "You're freaking barbarians, all of you! Let me go! I will not be your slave or Odin's breakfast!"

"I will not hurt you," he shouted.

But blood still ran from her wound. And she had probably increased the flow with all her kicking and screaming and struggling, because her voice trailed off, and her body went limp in his hands.

He looked at her from the side. She was pale but beautiful. Her eyelashes were long and thick, her nose straight and delicate, and her lips full and red like a strawberry. She was dressed in the strangest clothes he had ever seen. A short green jacket made of some strange green hide, slim black trousers, and big boots with thick soles. Witch or not, she needed help, and fast. He had to get her back to the village, to the healer they had brought with them.

Solver moaned and sat up, holding his head.

He'd be all right. Einar's concern now was this woman. He could pass her to one of his men to care for, but something about her—the way she had so fiercely spoken with Thorir, the strangeness of her, the beauty, the fact that she might be a real witch—made him hold on to her. He took the woman in his arms and carried her outside to the ship so that he could stop the bleeding with the small healing kit he had on board.

And try as hard as he could not to study those long eyelashes and that strawberry mouth and those long, sculpted legs.

# CHAPTER THREE

Mainland, Orkney, May 8, 880 AD

Holly woke up to a splitting headache. Her mouth was dry, and her whole body burned. She was lying on something soft and was covered with something warm and cozy. Around her were the muffled sounds of people talking, a knife clanking against wood, and soft steps. The scents of earth and stone and home cooking filled her nostrils.

Finally, she opened her heavy eyelids and looked around. The large room was dimly lit. Sunlight trickled in from a hole in the ceiling high above and a single broad door. And oil lamps hung on beams here and there. The walls were made of stones, and the floor was packed dirt covered with scattered reeds.

Holly lay in what seemed to be a bed in an alcove. In the center of the room was a long hearth, around which women and girls were cutting vegetables, kneading dough, and butchering meat.

Holly touched her head and her fingers landed on a bandage. How? Where was she?

Then she remembered.

Thorir Treebeard had slapped her so hard that she'd seen stars exploding, then he'd pushed her off the chair and hit her with it.

Then another Viking had grabbed her from behind, locking her arms so she could only kick and struggle against him.

Then everything had gone black. Did she have a concussion? She found the strength to move her hands over her body. She was still in her clothes, and so far, only the side of her arm was sore. Other than that, she felt fine.

Had that other Viking kidnapped her? It didn't seem like she was being kept against her will or anything, and at least they'd bandaged her wound.

Freaking time travel. Unbelievable. Please, let it be a hallucination. Or at least a dream.

But everything around her—the scents, the sounds, the feeling of her body—was all too real.

She sat up, panic gripping her lungs. The movement caused an explosion of pain in her head, but she ignored it, frantically looking around. It seemed as if she was still back in time, just in a different place. So even more time had passed since she'd appeared here...

She had a sudden, overwhelming longing for home. Her apartment, with its floor-to-ceiling windows, white furniture, and chrome finishings, always smelled like freshly ground coffee courtesy of the maid who came every day. And she missed the summery scent of her favorite watermelon air freshener sticks. She usually worked at home after dinner, mostly so that she wouldn't feel lonely in the spacious penthouse apartment. She'd put on some smooth jazz and pour herself a glass of red wine. It was always sunny and quiet, and the views of Lake Eola, the park with palms, and downtown Orlando were better than wall art, especially at sunset.

Here, everything was dark, cold, and smelled like animals and earth. Even her office at Sunnybeach Developments was all giant windows, modern furniture, and art.

*Oh God! My work!*

She might lose the merger. She needed to go back right away. She needed to find Ms. Verdandi or that damn tree or that golden spindle. The work of the last three years would go to waste. And her mom and dad, they'd be killing themselves with worry.

A tall, broad, dark shape appeared in the open doorway. She needed to escape before some other Viking decided to tie her up. Then the giant Viking who'd hauled her away from Treebeard's camp strode in. Fear tightened her muscles. He looked at her, and she grabbed the fur blanket, tugged it to her chin, and huddled in the corner of the alcove.

He stopped and studied her with a frown. When he'd stormed into Treebeard's tent, it had all been a blur, and she hadn't really gotten a good look at him. But now she could see him, and the sight made her stop breathing.

He was... "Huge" was the only word she could think of. Tall, like a lamppost, but not thin. On the contrary, he heaved with muscle. Thorir had looked big, but he was no comparison to this man. This man's shoulders were broad, the biceps under the sleeves of the pale-green tunic playing as he swung his arms. His chest muscles were broad. His hips were narrow, and his long legs were as muscled as those of a professional soccer player.

His hair was dark blond, almost brown, and a short beard covered the lower part of his jaw. He had full lips, as far as she could see, and big gray eyes under thick eyebrows. The very air around him was saturated with power and primal strength. He was so handsome that she couldn't think for a moment.

But she was still very aware of the ax in his belt, even though he didn't touch it.

He stopped before her alcove and put his hands on his waist, shielding her from the rest of the room. His gray eyes were dark and cold and burned into her skin as he studied her.

Holly lifted her chin.

"If you want to sacrifice me to Odin, you shouldn't have bandaged me."

He looked her up and down, his cold gaze unchanging, and Holly shivered a little.

"I do not intend to sacrifice you," he said, his voice a deep rumble.

"What then? Sell me into slavery?"

"No. Are you a slave?"

"Of course not."

"Are you a witch, then? A völva?"

Holly paused and pursed her lips. She hated to lie, but she was terrified. If she said she was a witch, would that keep him from selling or killing her?

"What makes you ask?" she said.

"I overheard Thorir call you that. Is it true?"

The best defense was offense.

"What do you care? You kidnap me, take me I have no idea where, and now, you're interrogating me? How do I know you won't treat me badly? How do I know you're not the enemy?"

Anger flashed across his face. In one smooth movement, he sat on the bed and grabbed both of her upper arms. He pulled her towards himself slightly, his eyes wide and furious.

"You are a guest in my land. I do not know you. I do not

know why Thorir thought you were a witch. I do not know what intentions you have towards my people. I will interrogate you until I get all the answers I need to decide if you are a threat or a friend. I must protect my daughter and this whole colony—from you, from the outlaws, and from any other threat. Now, answer me, who are you and how did Thorir know you are a witch?"

He was so close and so massive that Holly felt like a tiny toy he could snap in his hands. A deep, strangely invigorating vibration surged through her. She couldn't possibly be attracted to him, could she?

None of the guys she'd dated were like him. Not Ryan, her first love. Not Jack.

Jack, her last boyfriend, was a chef at a gourmet restaurant and had a bit of a round belly going on—which she didn't mind at all. It made him a little faulty, like her, and she'd felt more confident with him than with guys who flaunted their gym-perfect bodies. They'd even been living together and planning to have children—until he'd ditched her.

"Yes," she blurted out without really thinking. "I'm a witch. He saw me in Scotland while he raided a village and kidnapped me. You know the rest."

He let her go, and Holly breathed easier. He frowned. "You do not look like a völva. Why do you wear a man's clothes and a man's haircut?"

Holly gasped in indignation, touching her hair. "These are not a man's clothes, and this haircut costs a fortune!"

He frowned, clearly confused. "What?"

"I mean, I'm a woman, not a man. This is a fashion choice."

He looked her up and down and chuckled. "You have a strange sense of fashion. But that is not for me to judge. What I want to know is if you are from Sutherland."

Sutherland was the northern province in Scotland, she remembered.

"Yes," she said. Confessing that she had traveled in time was probably a mistake right now. She just needed him to relax around her, to allow her to move around freely. Then she'd try to find someone with a ship to take her back to Scotland.

Maybe even this man.

"What's your name?" she said.

"Einar."

"Einar," Holly echoed. "The descendant of Odin, fifty generations down?"

"Yes."

"Thorir is jealous of you, I think."

"Thorir is a worm, and I will rid these islands of him very soon."

Holly met his eyes. "Look, Einar, I don't mean you, your daughter, or any of your people harm. All I want is to go back home to Scotland. To Sutherland."

He nodded, still holding her in his stern gaze. "The only way is by ship. And I can spare none until I rid the Orkneys of outlaws. So it seems you must remain our guest for a time."

Holly frowned, desperate. "Why?"

"My priority is the safety of my people. Not a Scottish woman's wishes."

Irritation struck her, and her headache seemed to split her skull in half as heat rushed through her body. He turned to walk away, then looked back at her. "What is your name?"

She exhaled and shook her head. "Holly."

"Holly, unless you can make it worth my while to hire my ship and my men and go south, you are staying here. Besides, you still need to heal."

Make it worth his while? If she had some money or jewelry

or whatever these guys valued, she'd be on the next ship... But she had nothing. Damn it.

As he walked away, he threw over his shoulder, "If you know a spell to make me win, use it to help me purge these islands of Thorir Treebeard and his band of pirates, witch. Until then, you are stuck with me."

# CHAPTER FOUR

MAY 12

THE LONGSHIP MOVED through the wind quickly, the full sail flapping. Mainland, with its bare green hills and rocks, was fast approaching. The briny scent of salt water and seaweed was familiar and soothing. Their expedition to search out Treebeard on the island of Westray had been fruitless—the only sign being a freshly abandoned camp. After a day of chasing the seas, Einar was coming home empty-handed.

Ever-present Solver, the last person Einar wanted to speak to at this moment, came to the bow and stood next to him.

"Only a few days longer than a fortnight before King Harald expects you to be married."

Einar grunted in response.

"Do you have someone in mind?" Solver asked.

"All the women on the island are taken, old, or just little girls." Einar kept his eyes on the stone houses of the island.

"The witch is not," Solver said.

Einar raised his brows in surprise and looked at the man.

Solver continued, undaunted, "She is not too old, too young, or taken."

Solver winked. Einar snorted and shook his head. "Loki has taken your mind. My thanks to you, I needed a good jest after that useless day."

"This is not a jest."

Einar looked at him again, and Solver only raised one brow in response. Of course, Holly was beautiful, and although she was not a young woman, she was still very youthful. That flawless skin had no wrinkles. Her body looked strong and capable. And, although she was slim, she had curves his hands had ached to explore yesterday when he had sat on her bed and talked to her closely. Besides, she had a strong character—a very desirable quality for the wife of a chieftain or a jarl, which he would be once he married.

"She wants to go home to Sutherland. Maybe she already has a man who is looking for her now. How do you know she is not taken, anyway?"

"I asked her."

"Why would you ask her?"

"Because she is the only woman in the Orkneys who is not too old, too young, or taken."

Einar clenched his fist and hit the side of the ship. "I will not marry her. There is no way."

Einar had promised himself long ago that he wouldn't take another wife. He had his share of pleasures, of course. He was a man with needs. But he always made sure he did not spill his seed inside a willing servant girl or young widow.

He could not stand thinking that another woman would die, giving birth to his child.

A wife would want and expect children, too, whereas the

women he shared a bed with would be as keen to avoid pregnancy as he was.

"Then, I suppose I will go to Harald with the bad news, and you will need to go back to Rögnvald. Poor Svanhild, she just told me how she likes the island. She will have to get used to another disappointment."

Einar's stomach turned with guilt. He knew he was a bad father to her, and the poor girl was growing up without a mother. But he just could not imagine marrying again.

"I will not marry that woman. She does not want to stay."

Solver chuckled and sat back on the bench with a satisfied smile. "We shall see."

When they arrived home, Einar walked to the longhouse to see if Svanhild was all right. He may not be a great father, but he always needed to know she was alive and well.

He walked through the village, a gathering of stone houses left here by the Picts. Most of the houses were round and rather small compared to the wooden longhouses in Norway, where forests were abundant. His was the only stone longhouse built by Thorstein the Red. Wood was a rare resource here, so everything must be built from stone, which was freely available. Einar still had some wood left, but they needed to conserve the rare trees that grew on this rocky soil in this windy climate. He had to find some way to fuel fires for cooking and especially for warmth in winter. Somehow, the Picts, who had lived here before Vikings conquered these islands, had survived for hundreds of years. Einar would find a way for his people to survive, too.

He liked this new home. He liked being the chieftain here, and he would like being the jarl. He would build a community that would sustain itself, a prosperous jarldom, and he would be the jarl of the Orkneys. These would be his lands, and later, they would belong to Svanhild's children. He would ensure their future.

He had come to like the raw openness of the land and the sea that blew wind from all directions. There were good pastures for sheep and fertile soil where he could grow barley, oats, and vegetables.

He just needed a wife to keep these islands and ensure Svanhild's dowry. But how could he bring himself to marry again and risk the pain of loving and losing another woman?

Einar walked into the longhouse and, without meaning to, glanced at Holly's alcove. Svanhild sat there, and the two seemed to be involved in a conversation. Einar tensed, wary of Holly's intentions, ready to tear anyone apart who'd bring the slightest harm to his child. But the girl seemed to be enjoying herself.

Einar walked to them, still unsure, but stopped when the widest smile he had ever seen on Svanhild lit up her face. She looked so similar to her mother in that moment that his heart squeezed, and his eyes prickled. Between Holly and Svanhild, the gray cat that Svanhild called Loki walked back and forth, rubbing his side against Holly.

"I don't have a cat back home." He heard Holly say. "I work too much. The cat probably wouldn't recognize me once I got home."

"Is being a witch hard work?" Svanhild asked.

Holly rolled her eyes. "I do not work as a witch. I run a big company."

"Company? What is that, a jarldom? Are you a jarl's wife?"

"No, no." Holly laughed. "I'm single. I've read a lot researching my family, so I have a general idea of how things work here. A company is like when you build trade ships and a couple of smithies. You hire crews for the ships and blacksmiths for the smithies. And you send the ships full of...swords and knives and whatever else blacksmiths make...to sell them where people need them. Then you gather profit, pay your workers, and repeat."

"Oh, then you do a jarl's work, but you are a woman," Svanhild said, astonished.

Who was this woman?

Einar could not stand her strange influence anymore and made a few decisive steps towards them. They both looked at him, and the air changed completely. The smiles fell. Svanhild's face took on its familiar expression of wariness that she always wore when she was in his presence. Holly frowned and put her chin up slightly in stubborn defiance.

"That is enough, Svanhild," Einar said. "Go help the women with whatever they need."

"But I just brought Holly her meal. Bera, the healer, said she needs more food to gain her strength. She lost much blood."

His poor, kindhearted daughter. "Listen to your father, Svanhild. Go. You should not talk to people you do not know."

"But I want to hear about Sutherland—"

Agdis would have known how to talk to her. But he had no idea. He only knew how to command.

"Svanhild," Einar said.

The fire in her eyes died, and she looked down, compliant but angry underneath. "Yes, Father."

She stood up, turned to Holly, and said, "I shall leave Loki with you. He will keep you company while you are getting better."

Holly smiled broadly. "Thank you, Svanhild. That's very kind of you. Loki and I will be good friends."

Svanhild nodded and walked out. Holly petted the cat gently, and it rubbed against her hand. Einar had the strangest impulse to feel her hand brush against him like that, too.

He shook it off. Loki—the god himself, not the cat—was probably sitting on Solver's shoulder, whispering strange ideas. Because Einar was actually wondering if there was an agreement he could make with this woman.

But before that could happen, he needed to know more. He still did not trust her, especially after hearing the wild story she had just told his daughter.

"Are you recovering?" he asked.

He studied her face, which was still pale, and the big bruise that was forming on her high cheekbone. Seeing it made him want to follow Thorir to the depths of Helheim and destroy the bastard.

She leaned back on the wall. "I stood up today to go to the bathroom, so that's something. You have a very sweet daughter. Does she have a mother?"

Einar's jaw tightened. He still could not speak about Agdis without pain.

"She died a long time ago."

"Oh," Holly said. "I'm sorry. It must not be easy to raise a child on your own."

Not easy was an understatement, but not because of Svanhild. He just did not know how to be a good father. He was bound to lose the people who were close to him, and he could not bear losing the only child he had.

"Hm," he said. "Do you have family back in Sutherland?"

Her face fell. "Just my parents."

"You are a beautiful woman. No husband? No children?"

She raised her eyebrows in surprise and might have even blushed, but then she swallowed and looked down at her hands. Flashing a strangled smile, she said, "No."

Einar suppressed the urge to cup her jaw and tuck the lock of hair that had fallen over her face back behind her ear. To make her look at him with those beautiful eyes again. "Why not?"

She shook her head. "No luck, I suppose."

No luck for them. Big luck for him.

"Not even a betrothed?" he asked.

She smiled, amused. "What is this, a dating interview?"

"A what?"

"Never mind. I would like to marry, but I'm not sure it's in the cards for me."

"In the cards?"

"If destiny will allow it, I mean. I'm working too much. And also—well, just no luck. All my relationships ended in disasters. There must be something wrong with me that men prefer to run away from."

Einar chuckled. "I doubt that. You are a witch and a merchant? Never heard anything like that before."

But that did not mean it was not possible, he supposed. If she was telling the truth, she had skills that could be very useful to him here. He was getting more and more intrigued by her strength and her beauty. She must be a smart woman if she could do all that.

She cocked her head. "Trust me, many things in the past couple of days have surprised me as well. But all previous hostility aside, I wanted to thank you for saving me from Thorir and for allowing me to get well."

Their eyes locked, and he swore hers were the color of the pastures on the Orkneys. Beautiful, fresh, and so attractive.

He cleared his throat, chasing the feeling away.

He could not start feeling something for this woman, especially if he did end up marrying her.

"No need to thank me. I would have done that for anyone."

And with that, he turned and walked away before he could say or feel anything else that would put his heart in danger.

# CHAPTER FIVE

May 14

Holly walked out of the longhouse into the village and breathed in fresh cool air saturated with the scent of the sea and sun. She was glad she was finally strong enough to do more than just lie in her alcove, eat, steal glances at Einar, and talk to Svanhild. The village swarmed with morning activity. Two houses were being built out of stones, and people brought rocks and other construction materials on carts. Men hauled heavy sacks on their shoulders, and women carried water and milk in buckets, along with baskets of vegetables, flour, and sheep's wool. Voices spoke, hammers banged against rocks, and wheels thudded softly over the ground.

Holly's head was still heavy; although, it didn't hurt anymore. But according to her calculations, it had been nine days since she'd traveled in time. Normally, she would be boarding the plane to fly back to Orlando today. If she was not back on time, her COO Alan Murphy would sign the deal instead of her and take all the credit for her hard work.

And maybe even her position.

The position she had worked so hard for. The position that had pretty much put a stop to her personal life. The position a woman in construction rarely occupied.

Holly looked around and noticed ship masts down the hill. If Einar didn't want to give her a ship, maybe she'd find a captain who could be persuaded. She didn't know yet by what because all she had with her were her clothes—Thorir had taken everything else. But she'd figure something out.

Raising her chin and straightening her shoulders, she marched down the hill towards the ships. There were seven giant longships and several smaller ones, probably fishing boats. Obviously, she'd have a better chance of getting a small boat, but since she had no idea how long it would take them or if a small boat would be able to make it to Scotland at all, she needed to ask.

She spotted a man with long white hair and a weathered face sorting through fishing nets, and so she walked along the jetty to him, stopping before the boat.

"Hello there!" she said and waved her hand.

The man glanced at her and resumed his work. "Hello."

She coughed. "Do you rent your boat for hire?"

"Who is asking?"

"My name is Holly. I need to go to Sutherland."

He stopped and studied her, eyes narrowing. "Holly. Are you not the witch Jarl Einar rescued?"

Holly pressed her lips together. "I suppose I am."

"You do not look like a witch."

"It doesn't matter how I look. Can you take me there or not?"

He resumed his work. "I suppose I could."

Holly's chest filled with hope. She stepped closer to the boat. "Really? When?"

"But I will not."

Heavy steps thundered against the wooden planks of the jetty, and the fisherman looked to Holly's left.

"Because the jarl does not let boats leave without his permission."

The heavy footsteps stopped next to her, and a towering form shielded the sun. Holly cursed inwardly. She knew who it was without even looking. His very presence warmed the air as though he were the sun itself and sent her pulse racing a hundred miles per hour.

"I am not the jarl yet, Rokr," Einar said.

"You are to us."

"And you are right not to take this woman anywhere."

He grasped her by the upper arm and turned her to face him.

"You are not leaving. I forbade you."

Einar's gray eyes darkened like storm clouds, and Holly's lungs became hungry for air. She was surely just scared. It could not be because of the waves of tingling that his hand radiated from her arm through her whole body. It could not be the scent of him—surging sea, warm grass, tanned hides, and something masculine that belonged to him alone.

Something that turned her knees to water.

She shook her head. This was ridiculous. She needed to go back to Orlando and make the merger happen. "You forbade me? Am I a *prisoner*?" she asked.

His eyes were like granite now. "Of course not."

"Then, how dare you?"

He shook her slightly and pulled her closer. "I dare because I am the chieftain here. I dare because I need to keep my people safe, not send valuable ships to take a freed slave wherever she wishes. I dare because you are under my protection, too. And it is not safe for you to be traveling alone, especially with Thorir after you."

Holly jerked her arm from his grip and pushed him, but it was like trying to move a house. "I have to go now, or the work of the last three years will be ruined!"

Not just three years, actually. All A-grades at school, five years of killing herself at college, then that one internship at Sunnybeach Developments, which made her see that construction meant making something amazing out of chaos, rock, steel, glass, and cement. Making homes and workplaces for people. She had loved it right away.

She'd made it to the highest level in her career, even though the voice inside her head always made her doubt herself and double-check her decisions. She'd learned to be assertive and to negotiate and demand what she deserved.

But her personal life was a disaster. Every single day she lied to herself that she was good enough, that there was nothing wrong with her, but four failed relationships told her a different story. They said she might be attractive, smart, and kind, but once people got to know the real her, they took off.

"The strange company you were talking about?" Einar said. "I do not care if you lose your wealth. I need all of the boats here to look for pirates. We do not know how many are out there or how many will come to their aid. We need even the fishing boats until every single island is safe. The lives of my people are more important than your work."

"A stubborn bull!" Holly yelled and walked away from him. But he followed her, grabbed her arm, and turned her to face him. His touch was strong and warm, and heat went through her skin.

"I need you to promise me that you will not do anything to try to escape," he said.

Holly shook her head, anger roaring in her. She pulled away and continued walking. "I will promise no such thing," she yelled back over her shoulder.

"Then I will make you a prisoner," he said from just behind her.

Indignation burned through Holly like fire. "A prisoner?" She swung around to face him again.

They had arrived at the vegetable garden that was behind Einar's longhouse.

He loomed over her, light playing over the dark gold of his hair, his eyes cold. "You leave me no choice."

Before she could say anything, he stepped back and removed his tunic. Holly's jaw dropped as her eyes traveled over the mountainous muscles of his shoulders and biceps, the rolling hills of his pecs, and the flat planes of his six-pack slightly covered in hair. A Thor's hammer pendant hung from his neck. Holly's mouth dried like a puddle in the desert, and she forgot what she wanted to say. He turned his back to her, his muscles rolling like waves, and picked up a hoe that was leaning against the wall. Then he bent a little and began digging a narrow trench.

Holly breathed out, trying to shake herself out of the stupor the sight of his body had plunged her into. She didn't really believe he'd make her a prisoner. He wasn't that kind of man.

"Aren't you the chief here?" she asked. "Why are you doing manual labor?"

"Because I'd rather do this than sit on my arse, wait until winter comes, and then find out we have nothing stored in the cellar. The thralls must be busy in the oat field since no one is here. There aren't enough hands to do all the work."

Wow. Einar was not afraid to get his hands dirty. He really was dedicated to his people. She respected that. She felt the same way towards her company. When she had started as a sales manager, she'd decided to work on the construction site of one of the hotels in Orlando for a day. She'd just done unskilled work—pushed carts with dry cement, shoveled dirt, cleaned up rubble—but the experience had taught her what it was like, to be on that site, to build something that needed to be safe and solid and beautiful at the same time. She'd gained the highest respect for anyone who worked tough physical jobs.

And she thought Einar understood exactly what she had experienced.

She went to the wall, picked up another hoe, and began repeating his movements.

"I don't know much about gardening," she said. "What are you doing, exactly?"

"Preparing the soil to plant parsnips."

"Oh. Parsnips. I like parsnips."

"You do not need to do that," he said.

"No, no, this is actually good. I don't have any way to repay you and your people for saving me, feeding me, and tending to me. If I can help in some way, I'm happy to."

Einar shrugged one shoulder. "I suppose."

"I truly respect that you're doing this," she said. "I'd do the same in your place."

"But you are not a jarl, are you?"

"Not a jarl. But I do have quite a few people I'm responsible for. All I'm trying to say is, I understand where you're coming from. Thorir's bastards are no joke."

They continued to hoe in comfortable silence for a while, and Holly began wondering what else this stern, brave, gorgeous man was hiding under that austere profile. And what he was ready to risk for his people.

Out of nowhere, her head started spinning and her vision blurred. She dropped the hoe and sat down on the ground, hard. Einar came to her with a worried look. He took her by the shoulders, his naked, glistening torso right in front of her. Her breath caught.

"Are you all right?" he asked.

"Just a little dizziness. I'm fine."

"You're not entirely healed yet."

He sat next to her, and she appreciated his concern. She wanted to give him some comfort, too.

"Einar, you will succeed. You will free Orkney and the Shetland Islands from the outlaws. You will be one of the first jarls of the Orkneys, and you will establish a successful, noble Norse house that will rule for many generations."

He moved some dirt with the hoe. "I will?"

Holly sighed, a smile beginning to burn within her as she saw hope and relief on his face. "Yes. You will. You will have three sons."

Did he go pale suddenly, or did she imagine it?

"How do you know?" he asked, his voice strained. "Did you see it? Did the Norns whisper that to you?"

Holly let out a long breath. This was one of the random things she'd read while she was researching her genealogy.

She couldn't lie anymore. She wasn't a witch or whatever. And maybe he'd believe her and change his mind about keeping her here. Maybe he'd help her.

"No one whispered it to me, but I did see it. Or rather, I read about it in history books."

His eyes narrowed. "What?"

"I'm from the future, Einar. I'm not a witch. I'm from the twenty-first century, which is about eleven hundred years in the future. I traveled back in time when I touched a golden spindle in Scotland." He looked at her blankly. "I mean, in Sutherland. I landed during Thorir's raid, and he saw me appear out of nothing. He thinks I'm a witch, but I'm not. I'm a regular woman from the future, and I need your help to get back home. To return to my own time."

Einar studied her with a stony expression for a moment without speaking. One corner of his mouth twitched, then both corners crawled up. He smiled, and then his head fell back and he laughed. He laughed so loud and so hard, Holly was afraid the whole village would hear and gather around them. She'd never seen Einar laugh or smile before. She hadn't even imagined he was capable of it. He was especially handsome when he smiled, and she wished he would smile more often.

Ah, darn it. He didn't believe her.

"I don't blame you," Holly said. "It's a crazy explanation."

He wiped one eye and exhaled, then gave out one last chuckle. "You should be a skald instead of Solver. You are much funnier. Good jest, Holly. A witch with a sense of humor."

Still laughing and shaking his head, he stood up and returned to hoeing. "But you are staying here. Until I allow you to go."

Holly gasped, seething with anger. Although, strangely, the thought of spending more time with Einar brought a pleasant warmth to the pit of her stomach.

What was wrong with her that she was thinking about how nice it would be to spend time as a Viking's prisoner rather than getting back to what really mattered?

She could just imagine her mother saying, "I told you so. This trip was a bad idea."

And for the first time in her life, Holly couldn't agree with her mother more.

# CHAPTER SIX

May 17

Einar winced as he lifted the cup of mead to his mouth. The shallow wound on his shoulder from today's skirmish was still untreated, and it ached. He would deal with that wound and the rest of them later. He did not want to take Bera away from treating those with worse wounds.

The hall of his great longhouse also served as the mead hall, and his warriors sat around the small tables eating and drinking. The atmosphere was cheerful—they had found a small camp of outlaws on one of the northern islands and had been victorious today. Only a small number had escaped.

It was warm and pleasant in the orange-red lights of the hall, the air rich with the scents of meat, stew, fresh bread, and mead. Men talked, laughed, bantered, and discussed the fight.

"And then, Jarl, when you smacked that oaf in the face like a naughty boy, I would have shit my pants, had I not needed to send another one to Helheim."

Einar shook his head with a small smile. "Lofarr, I am not a jarl."

The man only waved his hand dismissively. "You will be. We are well on our way to relieving the islands of those bastards."

Einar clenched his teeth because that was only one condition. He was very far from fulfilling the second condition, the marriage. Days until the date were fast fleeing. Einar looked around the room for Holly, a habit he had developed since he'd brought her back from Thorir's camp. He saw her eating with Svanhild in another corner of the room, her face soft, a smile on her lips. Einar studied her beautiful features, the big eyes, the full lips, and the short hair that he had come to find strangely suited her.

She was a mystery. Something was very different and intriguing about her. He could see it, he could feel it, and he could even hear it in her voice. It was in the words she chose, the intonation of her speech, and the very postures of her body. He had never met anyone like her.

But then she looked directly at him, and their eyes locked. The room went quiet, people stopped moving, and everything but her eyes stopped existing. His heart drummed in his ears. Mead hit his blood hard and sent a warm buzz through his whole body.

"And you have a candidate to marry," Solver, who sat next to Einar, said.

Einar broke eye contact with Holly and threw an angry glance at Solver. "Stop this."

In fact, he was done with the feast and had no desire to listen to more jokes and goading. He rose from the bench, the cuts on his legs paining him.

"Good night," he said. "Do not drink till you cannot tell a pig apart from a woman."

He walked to the other end of the house, where his bedchamber had been built behind a thin wooden wall. It was the only chamber in the whole house. He stopped in front of a servant girl who was pouring mead into Holly's cup.

"Bring me clean water and linen, and ask Bera for some herbs for pain. Tell her it is for my wounds." Then he glanced at Svanhild. "Good night, daughter. Go to sleep soon."

"Good night, Father."

Without looking at or acknowledging Holly, he walked into his room and lay on his bed, his head full of those green eyes and that red hair and her words: "You will be one of the first jarls of the Orkneys. You will have three sons..."

And then Solver's voice, "You have a candidate to marry..."

He growled. Marry her? No, surely that was out of the question.

If not her, then who? Bera? Bera was sixty winters old.

After a while, someone knocked on the door. Without looking, he hung his legs from the bed and removed his tunic. "Finally," he said. "Put that water and the linen on the bed. What herbs did she give you?"

"Angelica," said the voice that had been haunting him since he first spoke with her.

Holly.

He turned. She stood by the door, wide-eyed, lips parted, and watching him.

"Why are you here?" he asked.

"To bring you this." She finally moved, putting the large clay bowl of water on the chest that stood by the wall. She laid the linens next to it and set a jug nearby.

"I asked the servant girl. You do not need to bring me anything."

She shrugged. "I know. I like to help. And I needed to talk to you."

Einar stood and took a step towards the chest to wet the linens and begin cleaning his wounds. But he stopped before Holly as the scent of her reached him: lavender and herbs and something flowery and feminine. They were alone, and her proximity brought blood to his loins. She was so close, just a half step away, and he itched to crush her against him and claim those full lips.

It was only because he had not had a woman for months, he told himself. It had nothing to do with her. He needed to stop.

He cleared his throat, bent, and sank one piece of linen into the water.

"What did you want?" he asked, as he started to wash his arm with the gash. Normally, it was a wife's work to care for her husband's small wounds. Agdis had done it very well. She had taken an interest in healing, and it was their special ritual. She would care for him, and they would make love afterwards if the wounds allowed.

"I had an idea. Sutherland is quite far, but maybe you could spare a fishing boat to take me to the closest Scottish coast? I could make my own way on foot from there."

He winced as the water reached the open flesh, but he needed to wash the dirt away.

"Let me," she said. "You're in pain. Lie down."

Their eyes met. She would be the first woman besides Agdis and Bera to do that. That would not be so bad. Let her care for his wounds. She was a witch. Maybe she would say a spell and help him sleep.

And even if not, he ached to feel those hands on him.

"As you wish." He gave her the wet cloth and lay on his bed. He put one arm behind his head and watched her from under his half-closed eyelids.

She nodded and rinsed the cloth in the water, then sat by his side and applied it to the wound on his shoulder. The pain stung him, and he closed his eyes.

"Sorry, was that too rough?" she said and resumed, but more gently. Warmth spread through Einar's skin where she touched him, despite the coldness of the water. He longed for a loving touch, for the connection of souls, for the care that it meant.

Not that Holly cared for him. But he could pretend she did.

"So how about it? You allow one fishing boat to take me to the nearest coast of Scotland. It's not far, I know. I remember from the maps."

He studied her. "Maps?"

"Yes. Maps. Drawings of land and sea from above. Do you know what I'm talking about?" she asked.

"Yes. I saw one in Jorvik when Rögnvald and I visited there. Ubba showed one to me. He discovered it at the king's treasury after the city had been taken. I found it useless."

"Hm. Well, in the future, they are quite advanced and really help to navigate—"

"Are you still insisting on the jest you told me the other day?"

She shot a quick look at him, then covered his shoulder wound with a fresh, dry piece of cloth and tied it. It felt good to have it taken care of.

"It was not a joke, Einar." She emptied the used water into the night pot, poured fresh water into the bowl, and took a clean cloth. When she had soaked it, she put it on his chest and gently swept it over his skin. The coolness was welcomed, and he ignored the small pinches of pain as she brushed against the bruises left by shields.

"Of course not," he said.

"Still, you haven't answered my question." He watched her eyes grow darker as she washed his chest. Now they were the color of a pine forest in the mountains of Møre. Her hand stopped in the middle of his chest, and she looked farther down his stomach. There was a scratch across his right side.

Her lips parted as her eyes crawled down his stomach to the very edge of his trousers, and then a little farther. Einar looked at the soft curves of her breasts hanging right above him, under the tight garment that wrapped around her body. She had been offered a more traditional dress, but she'd refused it and washed and repaired her clothes herself, insisting that she would not stay here for long anyway.

He was getting hard as she traced the piece of linen down his body towards the waist of his trousers, and he swallowed a moan of pleasure as not just the cloth brushed against him, but the warm edges of her fingers.

Oh, how he wished she would go on and undo his pants and wash him all over. And how he would kiss her and claim her for his own.

He reacted before he could stop himself.

He reached out with one hand and brushed her cheek. It was just as he imagined—the softest thing he'd ever felt. Her sweet freckles were like golden sand. She held her breath at his touch, and their eyes met—hers were now the color of deep moss, and he was sinking into them.

He took her by the upper arms, gently brought her to himself, and touched her lips with his. And just that smallest connection sent need roaring through his veins.

He whirled her around and pinned her to the bed, covering her with his body.

Her sweet face was underneath his, surprise and fire in her eyes. Her lips parted, and he watched the soft plushness of them, itching to taste them and nip at them and bite them.

And then she wrapped her arms around him and lifted her face to his.

He crushed his lips to hers, and they tasted like honey, melting under his mouth. The taste of her spurred his hunger and made him burn for more. Fire seethed through him as he parted her lips with his tongue and dipped into her mouth. He circled her tongue with his, teasing it and stroking against it, the hungry game making him harder and harder.

She responded with a hunger that matched his own, and her hips began grinding against his.

If he did not stop now, he would not be able to stop at all.

And as he brushed his hand down her chest and cupped her breast, she froze and pulled her head back, stopping the kiss. He frowned, disoriented, then leaned in to resume the kiss, but she evaded him.

"You will not distract me, Einar," she said. "Can you spare a ship to take me to the closest point on the Scottish coast?"

He breathed heavily, then groaned, frustrated that she had pulled away and angry at himself for starting this in the first place. Clearly, all she wanted was a way out.

He rose and sat on the bed, and she sat upright, too, her hair unruly, her lips a little swollen and dark.

Einar ached to resume their kiss, ached for her to stay. He closed his eyes for a moment, gathering his thoughts.

And then, he had an idea. Maybe it was all Solver's talk, or maybe it was the insatiable hunger that Holly roused deep within him.

"Yes," he said, his voice still low and thick from the desire that thundered in his veins. "I believe I can."

She beamed and covered his hand with hers.

"Oh thank you!"

"But you will do something for me in exchange. I told you, you must earn your passage."

Her face fell.

"I won't sleep with you for favors—I'm not a prostitute!"

"That is a pity. But it is not what I had in mind. Will you be my wife?"

Her brows crawled up to her hairline. "What?"

"Marry me. And I will personally escort you to the place you are so eager to go."

"Are you out of your mind?"

"King Harald will only allow me to be jarl and grant me the islands as property if I clear them of outlaws and if I marry. Solver is here to witness that I am wed by the next full moon. Then he will take the news to Harald. You will be free to go after that. There is no other suitable candidate. Every woman on the island is either too old, too young, or taken."

She rolled her eyes. "Gee, thanks for the charming proposal. How long till the full moon?"

"I think ten days or so. We will be wed in four days. Solver should be satisfied."

She sighed. "I needed to leave like yesterday!"

"This is the earliest you get."

She held his eyes for a moment and pursed her lips. "Can I trust you on this?" she asked.

"I give you my word. Anyone can tell you my word is stronger than iron. I swear I will take you back once Solver is gone, and you will be free of our marriage."

She sighed and kept studying him. "All right, Einar. I've always thought if I married someone, it would be because I loved the man." She swallowed and looked down at her hands, her eyes glistening with tears. "But I don't think that is ever going to happen to me. So, okay, I'll take you as a temporary husband."

He nodded, picked up the wet cloth she had thrown on the bed, and began wiping his other hand. And as his betrothed walked out of the room, his skin itched for her to stay. His heart jolted a little as she closed the door behind her.

Because even though he'd told her it would be a marriage in name only, in truth, he would have a hard time keeping his hands off her and keeping his mind free of her.

And eventually, letting her go forever.

# CHAPTER SEVEN

MAY 21

"HERE YOU GO, Holly, it is ready." Svanhild held a white-flower wreath out to Holly.

The girl was lovely with her amber-red hair and long-lashed big hazel eyes. She probably looked like her mom; although, Holly could see some resemblance to Einar in her face. Svanhild's expression was full of awe and adoration, and Holly's heart squeezed.

This girl didn't have a biological mother, just like Holly didn't. And Holly was about to become her stepmother, which was like an adoptive mother in a way. For a short time, but still.

And she was excited about having a child, even temporarily. Holly felt like she wanted to give the girl a hug.

Although the servants and cooks bustled about the hall with the last feast preparations, it felt like Holly and Svanhild were alone in the dimly lit mead hall. Most of the village gathered outside by the jetty, waiting for Holly to come to the ceremony.

The house was thick with the mouthwatering aromas of stew, grilled meat, and fresh bread. All of the casks of mead that had been stored for a while, had now been brought over to the hall. Tables and benches were brought from other houses so that the whole village could celebrate together. White-flower garlands hung on the columns and walls.

"Thank you, Svanhild." Holly smiled, brushed Svanhild's cheek, and put the wreath on her head.

She wore a simple, white, ankle-length linen shift and a white apron dress with beautiful silver brooches that held the straps. The brooches had a female figure in the middle of a circle, with her legs standing broadly apart. Holly wondered if it could be a mystical symbol.

Between the two brooches, strings with polished beads of white and cloudy glass and moonstones hung.

Holly wished she could see herself in the mirror, but there were none.

"You will be my new mother," Svanhild said and hugged Holly. "I don't remember my real mother."

Holly's chest tightened as she returned the embrace, tears stinging her eyes. She knew how that felt, to not know what her real mother looked like. That had been the big, dark shadow in the back of her psyche for her whole life. What was so wrong with her that her biological parents didn't want her?

Growing up, she'd felt like an outsider, like a broken thing pretending to fit in. That was why she'd wanted to have her own children—because she wanted to feel the sense of belonging that it seemed only a blood connection could forge. From the age of twelve—when her parents had told her she was adopted—she had felt like something invisible was broken inside of her. She wanted to give any child she had, a feeling of normality and wholeness.

Did Svanhild feel like that, too? Could she give that to Svanhild? Likely not. She couldn't bring herself to tell Svanhild that she'd be leaving at the first opportunity.

"Marriages like this," she said through a clenched throat, fighting her tears away, "when the two parties do not know each other, might not end well, dear. But whatever happens, your father loves you very much."

Svanhild looked confused. "But most marriages are arranged between a man and a woman who do not know each other."

These were certainly different times. Had she been born in Viking times, Holly would have been married off to someone, and her husband wouldn't have the option of abandoning her. She wouldn't wonder what was so wrong with her that every single man she had a relationship with chose to leave.

For better or for worse, she was about to get married. She had been looking forward to this day ever since she was a little girl. Was it ironic that the sole purpose of marrying Einar was so that she could leave him?

"Let's go," Holly said and straightened the wreath on her head with trembling hands.

"Are you nervous?" Svanhild asked as they both began walking towards the door.

Holly inhaled deeply and exhaled, trying to relieve the tension that squeezed her lungs and airways.

"I think so."

"Is it because you like my father? Or because you are afraid of him?"

Holly shook her hands to stop them from trembling. Good question. Why was she so nervous? She was nervous because, silly her, Einar made her feel like the sun was shining on her alone. When he'd saved her from Thorir, when he'd ensured that she was healed, when they'd talked and worked together in the garden, and then, finally, when he'd kissed her.

He was kind and big and brave, and he made her feel like the air she breathed held more joy and more life than it ever had before. He made her forget that something was wrong with her.

She was nervous because she was getting married.

She was nervous because, deep down, she hated that she had to make a choice between going back home and marrying a man she actually liked.

She was afraid that she was going to break her own heart by leaving a man and a child she was coming to care about very much.

Einar, a single dad with a wonderful daughter, was not only a gorgeous man who made her quiver in the most delicious way possible, but he was also someone she admired: strong, committed, and ready to risk everything for his people. A man of honor and a man of strength. A leader, she could tell.

And then their kiss... No one had ever kissed her like that. No one had ever made her want to get naked and jump on him right then and there just from one kiss.

What would happen once they were married?

No, she couldn't possibly agree to have sex with him. She needed to get a hold of herself. No matter how good his kiss had been, no matter how warm and pliable she felt in his strong hands, and no matter how excited she had been to feel his body pressed against hers, she would never allow it to go further than what was necessary for social appearance. A kiss, maybe. Or holding hands.

Holly straightened her back. "I'm not afraid of your father, Svanhild. Are you?"

Svanhild shrugged. "Maybe a little. I know he would never

hurt me. But I just do not know him. He is like a stranger who takes care of me and tells me what to do."

Holly wanted to say something, but at that moment, they reached the doors and opened them.

Outside, the wooden path towards the water was covered with the same small white flowers that were in Holly's wreath, and that decorated the house. Down below, by the jetty, men, women, and children looked up at her as Holly and Svanhild began descending towards them.

Holly looked for Einar, and she easily spotted his tall, massive, proud frame standing on the longship. By his side was Solver, who, Holly guessed, would probably lead the ceremony. The ship was decorated in flowers, as well.

Her heart drummed so hard that she thought it would break her ribs and jump out of her chest. Her feet wobbled. And then Einar's eyes found hers, and everything else ceased to exist.

It was as though the earth stopped turning, the wind stopped blowing, and people stopped breathing. All nervousness was gone from Holly's body, and instead, strength and confidence filled her. He was a rock, his eyes said. He had her. He'd always have her.

Holly didn't remember how she got there, but soon, she was by the ship, and Einar was helping her in. His fingers wrapped around hers. His skin was warm and calloused, his fingers big and strong. A wave of tingling went through her from his touch. Their eyes met, and she was swept into the stormy depths of his.

When they stood by the mast, Solver beamed.

"See, Einar, I told you. Listen to Solver. He knows."

Einar made a dubious "hm" sound and looked at Holly.

"Now, the betrothed, please join your hands," Solver said.

Einar took both of Holly's hands in his. The boat tilted

under her feet, but she didn't know if it was from a wave or from his touch. Solver wrapped a narrow white linen towel, embroidered with runes and Viking-style ornaments, around their hands.

"This towel is the symbol of ties that will unite you forever," Solver said. "In front of gods and in front of men, let us bless this union of Einar and Holly and wish them a long, prosperous, and fertile marriage."

Fertile? Holly's cheeks burned. Her stomach squeezed. She was likely a barren woman; although, she would have loved nothing more than to give birth. Einar must get married again after her if he ended up having three sons. But as she glanced at him, all thoughts evaporated. All of the connection that had previously been between them was gone. His eyes were ice-cold and panicked.

What had happened? She shook her head. She shouldn't care. This marriage would never be long or fertile in any case. Maybe he was just reminded of that.

"Do we have a sacrificial sow to receive Freyja's blessings?" Solver asked Einar.

"No," Einar said, his voice hard. "None of that is necessary. I doubt Freyja will bless us with children anyway."

It was as though he had slashed Holly with a knife. How did he know she couldn't have children?

"As you wish," Solver said. "Then, please say your vows now."

"I have no vows," Einar said.

Holly's heart sank. Yes, it would be a short marriage, but still, this stung. She wanted him to care. And all this told her was that, yet again, a man didn't want her. All she was for him was a means to an end.

The familiar pain of rejection crushed her to her core. Her mother's voice came, "I told you. No one will ever be interested in you if you behave this way. If you're too willful and too strong. No man wants a woman who is stubborn and independent."

"I have no vows, either," Holly said, trying to blink away tears.

Solver looked at his feet, uncomfortable. "Then it is time to exchange the rings and get you married. I believe there is a sword, Einar?"

Einar coughed. "Yes. There is." He walked to the nearest bench and picked up a beautiful sword in both hands. On the blade, two rings lay. "This sword belonged to my ancestors," Einar said when he returned to his place in front of Holly. "It is normally given to the bride so that she will give it to her sons once one of them can hold it. It will stay in the family. Usually, a bride would also give a groom her father's sword. But I understand you came with no possessions, so let this sword take both roles."

Solver nodded and picked up the rings while Einar laid the sword on Holly's stretched-out palms. She breathed heavily, the significance of the moment daunting.

"What do I do?" she whispered.

"Say, I accept this sword for our future sons," Solver said with a wink.

Holly thought she heard Einar's teeth grind against one another.

She raised her chin. They'd never have sons. "I accept this sword for our future sons," she said with a strong voice. Solver chuckled. He seemed to be the one enjoying this wedding ceremony the most.

"Put it on the bench, Holly. You will now exchange the rings," Solver said.

Holly did as was asked and turned to Einar. Solver held out both rings on the palm of his hand. They were simple silver rings, with the same ornate Viking pattern engraved along their circumference. Einar picked up the smaller ring and took Holly's left hand. Surprisingly gently, he put the ring on her finger.

"I take you as my wife," Einar said, his voice velvety, low, and intimate.

It reverberated through Holly's whole body and set a longing ache somewhere in her belly. Her pulse beat violently in her temples. She picked up the big ring, her hands shaking slightly. She took Einar's giant palm, the warmth of it burning her cold hand pleasantly.

"I take you as my husband, Einar," she said and put the ring on his finger.

Einar took her other hand, and they stood, looking into each other's eyes.

"Before the gods and before men, you two are now husband and wife!" Solver thundered. His voice carried across the water, and the crowd of people erupted in cheers. Holly's breath was so quick and loud that she thought her chest would explode. She was married. To Einar.

"Kiss your bride, Einar!" Solver cried, a giant smile on his face, shaking his fists in the air.

"That, I will gladly do," Einar said. Wrapping his arm around Holly's waist, he crushed her against him and sealed his mouth with hers.

As she sank into the sea of gentle torture that her husband's mouth inflicted on her, her head spun and her limbs went weak.

She'd just realized one of her lifelong dreams, to be married.

But it was nothing like what she'd imagined. And as delicious as Einar's kiss was, she couldn't help thinking this dream might just turn out to be a nightmare.

# CHAPTER EIGHT

"DO NOT EVEN THINK I want this any more than you do," Holly said through her teeth.

She sat by Einar's side at the bridal table. The hall rang with voices and was filled with the scents of food and mead. The feast had gone on for the whole day, and it was evening now. Einar was glad to see his people celebrate, their faces lit and their eyes already a little cloudy.

"Oh, I intend to enjoy this marriage fully," Einar said.

He was angry at the joy he felt about his marriage to Holly. Quite the opposite of the conflict roaring within, the atmosphere around him was cheerful, and from time to time, someone stood up and loudly proclaimed a toast and a blessing to the newlyweds. Svanhild, who sat by Einar's side, was playing with her cat and feeding it pieces of grilled meat from her bowl.

"What do you mean?" Holly looked at him, her face a mask of worry.

"You are my wife until you leave. And I am your husband. I

plan to savor what happens between a married couple in the bedchamber."

Holly's mouth dropped open, and Einar took a moment to enjoy her astonishment.

"You can forget it," she whispered.

"We shall see," Einar said. He would not force her into anything. But she responded to his kisses like fire to kindling, so he knew she wanted him. And his body ached to continue what they had started.

"Svanhild, stop feeding the beast from the table," Einar said. "You are teaching it that it can beg you for food anytime you eat."

"But he's hungry."

"He needs to learn he has his own place where he eats," Einar snapped. "Right there, by the door."

Svanhild's face fell, and Einar felt the sting of regret for being so harsh with her. He supposed he could have said it differently, but the tension within him had made him snap. He was angry that he had gone through with a marriage he did not want, terrified of how much he enjoyed the thought of Holly belonging only to him, and also angry at himself for wanting her. All of that boiled within him in a dangerous mixture. He tapped his foot under the table and poured one cup of mead after another down his throat, unable to stomach the thought of food.

"You need to be stricter with him, for his own good," Einar said, trying to make his voice softer.

"Yes, Father," Svanhild said and took the cat away.

Solver, who sat by Holly's side, stood up.

"This wedding is by no means usual," Solver said. "The bride did not have family by her side, so there was no traditional racing to the mead hall. We will never know if your family would have served mead the whole feast, Holly. We will never know the taste of the bridal mead that would be served for the whole month. But we do know that although you two have not known each other for long, Einar is ready to begin the wedding night right now."

The hall erupted in laughter and wolf howls. Einar clenched his fists on the table. Holly looked down.

"But I am a skald," Solver said. "And I would like to tell a story that might inspire some encouragement for your future."

He walked from behind the table and went to the middle of the room so that everyone could hear and see him.

"Sometimes the Norns weave us strange destinies that we first think are the worst things that could happen to us. I visited a jarl in Norway not too long ago, Jarl Sigurd Randversson. He is happily married to a woman named Donna."

Einar saw Holly lean forward.

"They have a mighty fortress, a prosperous village, and two young daughters. The women there share equal say as men in all matters. They also fight alongside the men if an enemy attacks. Sigurd first thought Donna was a goddess, but it turned out his wife traveled in time from the future, sent by a Norn."

Holly gasped, and without looking at Einar, clasped his hand on the table.

"So there are more of us," she whispered, her eyes wide.

"This is just a story," Einar growled, although a pleasant wave radiated from where their skin touched.

"Are there more?" Holly asked. "Women who traveled in time?"

Solver looked at her, his eyes sly. "Yes. I have met with Jarl Kolbjorn and his wife, Rachel. Jarl Hakon and his wife, Mia. And I have heard rumors of Jarl Andor and his wife, Cathy, but I have not visited them yet." A smile spread on his face. "I might meet more time travelers."

Holly turned to Einar. "See. I told you."

Einar shook his head. "He is just a skald. It is his duty to tell stories that people will remember."

Holly had just started to say something when Solver interrupted her.

"And now, I believe it is time to accompany the newlyweds to their marital bed and make sure the marriage is consummated."

Holly's eyes grew wide, and she jerked her hand back.

HOLLY COULDN'T BELIEVE it when Einar, completely calm, stood and helped her up. Solver, together with ten men or more, stood up as well. With cups of mead in their hands and howling like wolves, they followed Einar and her to the bedchamber.

"They aren't seriously expecting to watch us have sex?" Holly hissed, tugging her elbow out of Einar's grasp.

"Of course they are," Einar said without even twitching. "How else are they going to know that the marriage was consummated?"

In the bedchamber, small white flowers covered the furs, and all of the lamps were lit. The scent of lavender and freshly washed linen filled the room. Einar led Holly to the middle of the room and waited until everyone entered.

"Well, gentlemen, I'm not sure what you came for, because I'm not letting him or anyone else touch me," Holly said.

The men guffawed.

"She makes a good jest," Solver said to Einar.

"I'm not joking," Holly said.

Solver lost his smile. "Do you not want this marriage to

take place? Why did you go through the wedding ceremony then?"

Holly paled. "What?"

"If the marriage is not consummated, it is invalid," Einar said through gritted teeth. "If you refuse me, all this was in vain."

Holly swallowed and sucked in her breath, raggedly. "Oh."

She was not going to have sex with him. Especially if there were people watching. She was definitely out of place among these Vikings if they thought that was okay. And what about all these women Solver had mentioned—Donna, Rachel, Mia, and Cathy? If they had traveled in time and married Vikings, did they have to go through this, too?

No, it didn't matter. She would not.

She turned to Einar, her eyes filled with tears, her cheeks burning, and whispered, "Einar, if you want this marriage to be valid, please make them leave us. I'm not joking. Please, do this one thing for me. I can't..."

Einar caught her eyes, and the granite in his eyes softened. He lifted her chin gently and kissed her on the forehead. The gesture was surprisingly sweet and reassuring. "All right, Holly. Do not worry. All right," he said, and tension as heavy as a boulder left her shoulders. He had her back. Even though this was against the rules of his culture, he had her back.

Then he turned to the men. "You must leave, Solver. The marriage will be consummated, but not until you leave us."

The men protested drunkenly.

"My wife is from Sutherland. They do things differently there. She will not consummate the marriage unless we are alone."

Solver nodded. "Fair enough. Nothing is typical about this wedding anyway. Do you give your word?"

Einar held Solver's eyes for a long moment, then nodded.

"Let us go then."

Solver led the men out. The door closed behind them, and Holly was alone with Einar.

It had been warm before, from the embarrassment and fear that had gripped her and boiled within her, but now it felt as though the temperature in the room rose to a whole new level. Einar crossed his arms over his chest and held her in his powerful gaze.

"Nothing and no one will harm you or do anything against your will, as long as I have a say in it," he said. "Do you understand?"

Holly chuckled. "Except for holding me prisoner on your island."

"You know the reasons for that. It is not to hold you here."

Holly nodded. She sighed deeply, trying to shake off the tension that Einar's presence caused in her.

"Besides, soon you will be gone," Einar said, his voice hoarse.

Holly's throat thickened.

"Would you like mead?" He nodded to the jug and two cups standing on the little table.

"No," she said. "I've been drinking all day."

Einar was gorgeous in his white tunic, which streamed down the carved muscles on his chest and around his strong arms. A red belt hugged his waist, highlighting his narrow hips. His long legs stood proudly apart in his soft leather boots. His hair was combed and groomed. His eyes were dark and intense. The air in the room thickened, as if an invisible cloud charged with electricity between them. Holly couldn't move or say a word, or she knew she would give in and fly into his arms. And then she would be truly lost...

"I am not going to lie, Holly," he said. "I want you. I want my wife. And I have every right to make you mine tonight."

He took a step towards her, and Holly's mouth parted, the words sending her mind spinning like a carousel.

"I will not do anything you do not want," he said. "But let me try to persuade you."

He took another step and grasped her hand in his, the hot, dry skin of his fingers scorching her, the very touch so exciting, her stomach flipped.

Would it be so wrong to sleep with her husband on her wedding night? What if this was the only one she'd ever get?

Considering her history with men, that was likely exactly what was going to happen.

And yet here he was, the most handsome man she'd ever met—a kind man, a responsible man, a man whose body made her heart stop beating—and he wanted her. And there was no risk of him leaving her because she'd be leaving him soon anyway.

Besides, she wanted this. She wanted it so much, her nipples ached at the thought of his lips and his hands on her body, and of him inside of her.

"Okay," she said. "Try."

# CHAPTER NINE

THE CORNERS of his mouth crawled up as he gave a lazy, mischievous chuckle that melted Holly's joints like butter. He tugged her hand and drew her closer, his other arm wrapping around her waist and crushing her to himself. The pressure of his hard body against hers made her nipples harden to stiff peaks.

Oh God, just the way he smelled—leather, linen, and clean skin—made Holly's heart pound frantically.

"You are going to undress," he said. "Then I am going to make you mine. And you are going to tell me if you want it slow and gentle...or hard."

His voice purred, reverberating in her rib cage like the distant rumble of a coming storm.

"Say yes," he said.

"Yes," she managed, the word flying at the edge of her breath.

He kissed her, his lips gentle and probing at first. He nipped her lower lip, soft and warm. Then, gently, he parted her lips with his tongue and began dipping in with deep, hot strokes.

His kiss was like an expensive, old, smoky scotch. It had so many undertones and tastes, and she wanted more. She wrapped her arms around his neck and drew him closer. The taste of him, the smell of him, the feel of him, sent a shudder of electricity through her.

He pulled her even closer and ran his hands up and down her back, then one hand glided into her hair and tilted her head. His mouth left hers, and he dragged his lips down her chin, down her neck, leaving soft, wet kisses. His short beard scraped tenderly against her oversensitive skin.

He reached the edge of her shift, hooked it, and said, "Take this off before I tear it to pieces."

Holly's chest rose and fell. No one had ever been so bossy with her. She was the one who issued commands all day long at work, and it might have transferred to the bedroom.

Einar's possessiveness, his control, the intensity in his voice, and his predatory gaze, crashed over her like a wave of pleasant disorientation. Like he had undone some sort of tie within her, and she had begun softening. Opening up.

She released the brooches and let the apron dress slide down her body and pool around her feet. Then she untangled the straps that held the shift at the base of her neck and pulled it off her shoulders.

She paused. She was about to stand only in her panties in front of Einar, and there wouldn't be any way back. She felt as though she was at the edge of the Grand Canyon, wind howling around her, and sand and rocks shifting under her feet into the abyss. Just one step into the unknown and she'd be gone.

Something hollow and heavy ached in the center of her body, needy and hot. She wanted this too much. This would be just for a few days. She wouldn't give him the power to hurt her, to reject her.

Holly took a deep breath and pulled one shoulder of the shift down, then the other. She watched Einar's eyes grow darker as she dragged the shift down and finally let it fall on top of the apron dress. His eyes inched over her naked skin, glistening as though he had just seen a sunrise for the first time in his life.

"How beautiful you are, Holly," he said, almost in a whisper.

He stepped towards her and stroked her shoulders gently, then moved down her arms, warming her. Then he touched her hips, and without warning, hooked his hands under her butt, lifted her up, let her legs wrap around his waist and lock behind his back, and carried her to bed.

The gesture was so unexpected and so hot. The touch of her sex, through the thin material of her panties, against the linen of his tunic and the hard muscles of his stomach behind it, his broad body between her hips—it gave the feel of what it would be like to have him on top of her, between her legs.

He laid her on the bed, and she sank into the silky softness of the furs.

"How do you want me?" he asked.

Her breath disappeared at that. How could he be so possessive and yet give her all the control?

"Hard," she said. She longed to feel his weight on her, his muscles gliding against her, him inside her. "I want you..."

"I am here to please," he murmured and removed his tunic. Holly bit her lip as his glorious body stood before her, tall and broad-shouldered, and narrow hipped, all hard muscles. He knelt before the bed and settled between her legs, grasping her hips and shifting her towards him. Then his warm hands were on her inner thighs, and he glided them slowly, massaging the flesh at the same time. They spread warmth and excitement through her legs, right down to her toes.

When his fingers reached her underwear, he said, "This is a strange garment." He eyed her panties curiously before pushing the fabric to the side. Holly's inner muscles clenched deliciously, anticipating his touch. He gently opened her folds and sealed his mouth with her sex.

She gasped and arched her back. Her hands curled around the furs in fists. A shudder ran through her. Her skin burned as though he'd set it on fire.

"Einar, oh, Einar," she moaned. "Oh God!"

He continued playing with her. Then he slid one finger inside her, and she was gone, losing herself in the decadent game he began to play. Her muscles tightened around him, her blood sizzling, her lungs too small to breathe. She might have begun moaning—she only heard his groans, which reverberated through her body.

She began grinding against his mouth, her hips going in a small circular dance and her breathing and moans so fast. She was close. She was about to—

But he stopped, withdrew.

"Odin and Freyja, what are you doing to me?" he rumbled as he was undoing his pants.

There was a giant bulge between his legs, and when he pulled his pants off, his erection jutted up, thick and long, and so delicious that Holly's muscles ached.

"I will make you mine," he said, kneeling on the bed between her legs. He slid her panties down her legs and threw them on the floor. "Now."

"Oh, make me yours," she whispered, her whole body small and feminine and so ready for him.

She glided her hands over his hard chest, down his stomach, then up again and into his hair... His hair was so soft and silky, and a little curly.

He kissed her again, claiming her hungrily, his breath

labored and ragged. He palmed his erection and nudged against her sleek entrance. Holly wrapped her legs around his waist, digging her heels into his rock-hard butt to urge him inside.

And then, with one swift movement, he invaded her, stretching her, opening her up, burying himself to the root within her. Holly gasped and arched into him, pleasure rolling over her like the tide.

He withdrew slowly and then thrust his hips again, and a helpless moan of pleasure emerged in Holly's stomach and rose through her throat. He thrust again, long. Then again, and again.

He rose to his knees and tugged her hips after him, so that they were connected, her hips now higher than her chest.

He sank into her again and again, never taking his eyes off her. It was as though he devoured her whole, with his eyes and with his body. He was enjoying having her for his pleasure, and yet there was something in his eyes, like pain, or like care.

As though he was holding back.

"Don't hold back," Holly moaned, her hips meeting his thrusts.

He put one hand on her clit, pinching it gently. A jolt of sweetness ran through Holly, and her inner muscles tightened around him, on the verge of an orgasm.

"You like that, my sweet witch," he groaned, tilting his head back, his fingers brushing her clit in broader strokes, his other hand still holding her in place.

His thrusts grew harder, tighter, and Holly knew he wouldn't last long, either.

Tension and heaviness built to an unbearable pitch, heat spreading within her.

"Oh, Einar, I'm—"

The orgasm blasted through her like a tornado, whirling her like a leaf in the wind.

Her inner muscles clenched, milking him.

"Oh, Holly," he whispered, his voice raw. "Oh wait—Damnation—"

He grasped her with both hands and thrust her onto himself as he convulsed, crying out in deep, throaty groans.

As Holly was still shuddering with her release, he fell on top of her, continuing to thrust as the last of his pleasure spilled inside of her. The waves of clenching ran through Holly, gentler now, and she wrapped her arms and legs around him, bringing him even tighter into her embrace. His head was buried in her hair, his breath deep and hot against her skin. They were both sweaty, but Holly didn't care. She'd take this kind of sweaty every day, multiple times per day.

She exhaled slowly and smiled, looking forward to cuddling with her husband.

Her husband. She was living in a strange, conflicted, but happy-for-now dream. Like a role-playing game or something.

A role-playing game she had started to really enjoy.

She had just made love to her husband—

Einar rose to his knees, and Holly opened her mouth to say that she was looking forward to spending every night like this until the very last day she was here, when she saw his face.

It was a stone mask, his eyes dark, his mouth a tight line. He didn't even look her in the eyes.

"What's wrong?" Holly asked.

"You," he spat. And when he met her gaze, his eyes threw lightning bolts at her.

Holly suddenly felt fragile, unprotected, and had an urge to cover herself. "What did I do?"

"You let me spill my seed in you."

Holly sat up. "I didn't make you do that."

"Yes, you did. You were too sweet, too good in my hands. You bewitched me. I have not spilled my seed in a woman since my late wife. I have sworn I do not want more children."

Holly stood up from the bed and went to her clothes. She put the shift on, needing some sort of protection, both physical and emotional. She was so silly. *Husband.* He was just a stranger.

"I had no idea. You should have told me. Besides, I didn't force you to come inside of me. If I knew, I'd have told you or helped you somehow."

He shook his head. "It was just too good. I could not control myself. I can always control myself."

She came to sit on the bed, wanting to comfort him. He was still naked, sitting without shame in all his glory. Her throat went dry at the sight of him.

"Look, Einar," she said. "If you're worried I might get pregnant, you shouldn't. I'm most likely incapable of having children anyway."

The words, said out loud, were like a boulder crushing her. Her voice must have given away her pain because Einar studied her with a frown.

"How do you know?"

"I've tried, multiple times. Insemination, you know, with doctors and stuff. It's even more reliable than normal sex. And still, nada."

He sighed and stood up, then began dressing. "That might be for the best," he said before walking out.

"What?" Holly said to the closed door.

# CHAPTER TEN

After Einar left Holly, he let Solver know that the marriage had been consummated, which interrupted the skald's drunken song and caused an eruption of cheers and howls through the room.

"Your chief will be jarl!" Solver yelled above the noise. "Jarl Einar of Orkney!"

His people clunked the horns and cups of mead and cried and jumped. But Einar could not join in their celebration. He stormed out of the hall under their weak protests, which were swallowed by more cheers.

He might have just condemned Holly to death in childbirth—and his future child—when he had sworn to himself that he would never do that again.

The night was chilly, but the frigid air was exactly what he needed to cool his thoughts. From the west, the horizon above the sea still glowed with dying hues of pink, violet, and orange. As Einar marched through the dark village, the smells of food and mead lessened, and the air grew rich with the scents of grass, sea, and damp soil. A short distance from the village, a herd of sheep that had been grazing during the day on the slope of a high hill were now sleeping. A sheepdog barked quietly as he approached but wagged its tail as it recognized Einar, and settled back to rest.

The sheep slept on, undisturbed. Around them, crickets chirped, and flies and mosquitoes circled lazily.

This company would do him. Maybe he would fall asleep, but he doubted it. He settled in the grass and watched the horizon for a few moments, then lay on his back and stared into the endless sky sprinkled with stars like white sand.

Was that Asgard, the world where the gods lived, and Valhalla waited for the brave? Did Odin see him from there? Did Freyja?

Was it the goddess of love who had possessed him tonight to find his release within Holly?

Einar looked for another explanation for why he could not stop himself, why he could not withdraw when for the last eight years, he had done exactly that with other women.

Unless the answer was not the goddess Freyja, Holly's magic, or anything supernatural.

The answer was that she was too sweet. That he had not wanted to stop. He'd loved sinking into her again and again. She'd fit like a good sheath. And he'd felt as though he made love not in Midgard, on a wooden bed in a simple house, but in the land of elves and gods. It had been like making love to a goddess.

It had felt better than mead, better than a freshly grilled boar made using his mother's recipe. It had been better than inhaling the scent of a fresh harvest.

And he could not stop.

His mistake, but Holly might pay for it with her life.

Einar reached for the three pendants that hung around his neck. One was a silver Mjölnir, the Thor's hammer pendant that every Norseman wore for protection. The second was a cat carved from walrus tusk, the pendant that Agdis had given him. The cat was a symbol of home, of a household where everything ran smoothly. She'd said it was so that he'd always come back home to her.

The third one was a carved rune on a small birch circle, ᚹ, *wunjo*, which meant "joy." He had carved it the day Svanhild was born, because never in his life had he felt such overwhelming happiness than when he'd held the little bundle containing his daughter. It was as though he was ready to hug the whole world.

The metal, the bone, and the wood felt reassuring under his fingers. Like he could absorb strength and support from them. Clear his head of Holly.

He hated knowing that she was going to leave and he would never know if she died or if he would have another child.

And even worse was, he did not want to stop making love to her. Talking to her. Watching her talk to Svanhild. Locking his eyes with hers and feeling like everything around them ceased to exist.

Einar lay there the whole night, desperately trying to sleep. But just like most nights for the past eight years, sleep evaded him. He'd finally closed his eyes just before the sunrise, and the shepherds had already come and woken him up with their voices. He rose, surprising them, and went back to his house, which was undoubtedly stinking with spilled mead and the sweat of people sleeping in the closed room.

But he did not make it to the house because his wife, dressed in her strange man's clothes, was marching towards him with a determined—if not angry—stride.

She stopped in front of him, pale-faced and beautiful, dark

circles under her eyes. Likely, she had not gotten much more sleep than he. Her eyebrows snapped together.

"There you are," she said. "I was looking for you everywhere. Where were you, husband?"

She spat the last word out bitterly, and her voice shook and broke a little. Had she been hurt by him leaving her alone? The thought was unsettling, and he pressed his lips together tighter. He should not care whether she was hurt or happy. This was not a real marriage, and it would end soon.

"Did you miss me in bed, wife?" he said to hide the small sting of guilt.

"Yes," she said.

Einar blinked. He had not expected her to say that.

"But only because I wanted to make sure you were alive. That you hadn't drowned in mead, or that wolves hadn't eaten you alive."

He sighed, almost relieved. For a moment, he'd thought she'd actually wanted him to stay with her as a real husband would. But this was better. Better to keep things between them at a distance. "What did you want?" he asked.

She lifted her chin, a barely noticeable expression of hurt behind her eyes. "I fulfilled my obligation. I married you. We consummated the marriage. Can you send me home now?"

Of course. She could not wait to escape from him. "Now?"

"Yes. Today."

"I told you. After Solver leaves."

"Well, make him leave today."

Einar shook his head. "I cannot send a guest away if I want to be a good host. Especially not the king's man."

She blinked, crossed her arms over her chest, and tapped one finger against her arm.

"Then lie. Find a reason."

He studied her. "What changed? Yesterday, you were ready to wait until he left."

Her cheeks reddened. "Yesterday, I thought I was entering an agreement with a decent man. But last night, he left me feeling like a used towel he'd jerked off into."

As she said that, her eyes filled with tears, and Einar longed to take her into his arms and kiss them away.

"And I really do not need another man to treat me like that. Even if I'm never going to see him again."

If Loki took a shit after eating a rotten troll, Einar could not possibly feel worse than that shit. Yes, he had behaved despicably for abandoning her like that after what they had together. An honorable man would never even treat a bed slave like that. Not to mention, his own wife.

Without meaning to, Einar reached out and clasped her hand, which she'd tucked between her arm and her chest. Her skin was cold and smooth, like polished stone.

"I never meant for you to feel like this, Holly. You are not a used towel. You are helping me keep this land and these people safe by being my wife. I abandoned you because of a pain in my heart that has nothing to do with you."

Her eyes widened, and she blinked several times.

She shook her head, her face softer now. "We all have wounds in our hearts that do not heal properly."

He covered her hand with both his palms. "I cannot send Solver away until he leaves on his own. And you cannot leave before that, or this was all for nothing."

She sucked in a breath and looked at his hands holding hers, then nodded. "Okay. But you must promise not to be a jerk like that again. And don't you dare disappear in the night."

He released her hands. Her words amused him—she sounded like a real wife. "Woman, know your place," he said, turning and walking towards the longhouse. She followed him.

People began coming out onto the streets and greeted him and Holly, their faces friendly and cheerful. "I promise I will treat you with honor as long as you deserve it. But I will not answer you about my whereabouts."

"Where were you, anyway?" she asked, as if she had not heard his words.

"Just slept with the sheep."

"Well, don't sleep with the sheep tonight. Stay in your bed. With me."

Einar nodded. Deep inside, he looked forward to being in the same bed as her. And he hated himself for it.

# CHAPTER ELEVEN

May 25

Holly woke up squeezed under a furnace-hot arm and leg as heavy as trees. It was still dark and quiet, so it was probably the middle of the night, but her bladder was full. She needed to go to the outhouse. Reluctant to go into the cold, she nestled against Einar, absorbing his weight and inhaling his now-familiar scent. He stirred and pulled her into his embrace.

Her husband.

Not really. She was just pretending, playing at marriage like a little girl. Oh, was it so wrong that she enjoyed this marriage so much?

They made love every night, but he never came inside her again. She longed for him to—the satisfaction of their common release had been earth-shattering. She wanted more. She had compulsions, like finishing a box of chocolates if she started one or binge-watching a series through the night even though she had meetings all morning.

This desire was much worse.

But it was his rule, and she respected it.

Holly squirmed as she became uncomfortable. She needed to pee. She glanced at Einar, who slept peacefully, his usually stern profile relaxed now, making him look much younger. She stopped herself from reaching out and brushing her fingertips along his face.

He'd told her about his insomnia, but she hadn't noticed any signs of it. Ever since they'd started sharing a bed, he was usually sleeping when she woke up in the mornings. When he was awake, he pushed his erection into her hip and made her change her mind about hating morning sex.

Holly rolled out of his embrace and stood up, dressed in her linen shift, and walked from the bedchamber into the sleeping, wheezing main hall. Huddled in their alcoves, guests, servants, and Svanhild rested.

Holly hurried outside. The sky had begun brightening over the horizon, and the village would be stirring in a few hours.

When she left the outhouse, a quick rustle of grass made her freeze and turn. The wind? She narrowed her eyes to look at the dark hill spotted with the grayish silhouettes of sleeping sheep. They had been moved closer to the houses yesterday, as there was more fresh grass to graze. She heard another rustle and a pained whimper, then silence.

Then she saw them, and her blood stood still. Dark figures lurked among the herd of sheep, moving towards the village. And she heard disturbed *baa*s as a few of the figures herded the animals away.

Holly sank back into the grass. The men were getting closer to the houses. She could see axes and swords in their hands, and then light flared as the men at the front lit their torches.

She needed to alert Einar. Staying low, she turned and slunk into the house, praying the raiders wouldn't notice her.

In the bedchamber, she shook him. “Einar! Einar!”

His eyes snapped open, and he sat up, a dagger in his hand. “What?”

“I think we are being raided,” she said in a loud whisper.

“What? What did you see?”

“A group of men, very close to the village. They’re armed and have torches.”

Einar’s expression hardened. He leaped up and yanked on his trousers, then grabbed his sword and ax.

“Outlaws,” he said, his gray eyes black in the semidarkness. “I will alert the men. Stay here.”

But Holly couldn’t. She followed him, her heart pounding, her pulse beating in her ears.

Einar stopped in the middle of the room and said, “People. Wake up. We are being raided.” His voice was calm but loud, and it carried to every corner. People stirred, sitting up. “Women and children, stay inside. Men, take your weapons and follow me without a sound.”

The rustle of clothes and soft clanking of metal ran through the room as men dressed and took their weapons. Holly half expected the women to scream and the men to curse and spit. But these Vikings didn’t panic. They just did what needed to be done, what their chieftain said. Most people from her time would flip out. But these people were as strong and calm as stones. Holly respected them even more.

Was Svanhild calm, too? Holly found her alcove and sat by her side. The girl sat upright, watching everyone with wide eyes. Strong, brave little girl. Holly covered Svanhild’s hand with hers to reassure her.

When the men were out of the door, Svanhild hung her legs from the bed and found her apron dress.

“What are you doing?” Holly said. “We should stay inside.”

"My cat, Loki," Svanhild said. "He must have run away. I need to find him."

"Svanhild, they are not looking for a cat to steal."

"But he might get hurt in the fight."

Dressed now, she headed to the doors without taking a second look at Holly.

"Svanhild!" Holly called, but the girl was already outside. Holly cursed under her breath and followed her.

The day was already much brighter, and Holly could see the sheep being herded to the other side of the hill. She saw Svanhild looking around. Down the path, Einar crouched close to the house, surrounded by his men—forty or fifty of them, talking quietly. He was still shirtless, and Holly's heart squeezed at the fearless vulnerability of his mighty body. Staying low, they moved towards the pasture. She couldn't see any of the enemies nearby—were they hiding, already in the village? Or had they decided to just take the sheep? She doubted that.

Holly crouched next to Svanhild. "Look, they're about to fight. I'm sure Loki's somewhere in the house. Come back inside."

But Svanhild peered between the houses. "There he is! Loki!" She ran towards a small silhouette that immediately darted away.

"Oh damn!" Holly cursed and launched herself after the girl.

She could see the stupid cat running past a house and darting behind a corner.

"Svanhild, stop!" Holly yelled, her heart pounding from fear and worry. If any of the raiders were nearby... "The cat will be fine! Come back."

But Svanhild kept calling and running after Loki. Up the hill, behind the houses, screams, groans, and the clanging of metal against metal cut through the air. Holly glanced up. The battle had begun. She spotted Einar's bare back as he slashed his enemies. And she saw Svanhild running closer and closer to the battle.

"Svanhild, stop!" Holly called again.

"There!" Svanhild exclaimed, sinking to the ground. "Got you!"

Holly stopped by her side, panting. Oh thank God! In her arms, the girl held the little devil disguised as a kitten and pressed it to her chest.

"Okay, let's go back now," Holly said, looking for Einar to make sure he was safe.

The men were so close she could distinguish faces. Thirty feet away from her, she saw someone who turned her blood to ice.

The shaved head with the long braid, the tattoos, and the beard as bushy as the canopy of a tree.

Thorir Treebeard fought and killed one of Einar's men.

The first sunrays touched Holly's face just as Thorir glanced up, looking right at her.

His face stretched in surprise. Then his eyes narrowed like a predator's, his upper lip curled, and he lowered his head, looking at her from under his brows.

He started walking towards her, then sprinted like a wolf after its prey.

"Run, Svanhild! Run!" Holly cried, fear clasping her muscles like a cold vise. If he caught Svanhild... If he knew she was Einar's daughter... Terror weighed her whole body down, her airways closing, her vision darkening. She grabbed Svanhild by the neck of her shift and pulled her along. "Quick!"

But a horn blew, long and somber, then another, half as long. Holly looked back. Thorir stood and stared at her.

"Wiiiiiiiitch!" he roared, and everyone looked at him.

Holly tripped and fell. She jumped to her feet again, shoving Svanhild behind her back.

Thorir slowly raised his bloody ax and pointed at her. "Odin is still waiting for his sacrifice. And I will deliver you to him soon."

Then he turned and ran, along with everyone from his band. Einar and his men followed them, throwing axes and spears at them, but the enemies retreated too quickly.

Holly leaned down and pressed her hands against her knees, her lungs exploding from the running and the terror of seeing Thorir. She watched him until he disappeared behind a large rock.

The promise of her death hung in the air like a dark cloud. What a crazy life this was. No one hunted her in the twenty-first century.

"Now that he knows I'm here, he'll be back for me," she said, without realizing. "Oh God, I'm putting you and Einar in even more danger. I have to get away."

Holly's chest ached, knowing she couldn't stay with Einar and Svanhild any longer. She needed to get back to her own time, whatever it took.

# CHAPTER TWELVE

May 28

Following the raid, Einar searched through the island every day looking for Thorir and his men, but he found no traces. Einar had seen Thorir running away, and several of Einar's men had confirmed that the bastard and some of his warriors had not boarded their ship. So a number of outlaws must still be on the island. But it was as though they had dissolved into the giant hills and rocks and occasional bushes.

There were no remains of campfires, no traces of hunting or dressing game, no signs of anyone foreign on the island. Rain that had settled in since the raid certainly did not help, washing away any tracks. Each day, Einar returned home wet, tired, and angry, but the thought of Holly waiting for him warmed him like fire on a cold winter night.

Since the raid, Einar had put more men on guard duty, and they watched the village day and night. He forbade anyone to go outside the village alone, and women were only allowed if accompanied by men. Swords and axes became everyone's companions.

People grew quiet, the joy after the wedding washed away by wariness and fear. People watched the streets and the rolling hills behind the village for any signs of threat.

Tonight, the dining hall did not hum with voices. Einar's men exchanged few words as they ate. Einar watched Holly pour mead for Solver, who sat close to Einar in the seat offered to honorable guests. Solver looked up and thanked her and made a joke, no doubt something about a happy marriage. She smiled back, and although Einar did not have good reason, jealousy stung him. If he was honest with himself, he did not want her to smile at any man but him.

She made him feel better with her presence alone. He could sleep at night next to her—there was something so soothing and safe about her. Maybe because he knew this relationship would end, he could be himself by her side.

She was the perfect wife. She did not want children from him, nor could she have any. But she was always eager for him to take her. Holly even got involved in the household duties, which he did not expect of her given she would be gone soon anyway. She was smart, kind, and had a good grip on the servants, giving them clear commands. They respected her and accepted her authority eagerly. He could see leading people was not new to her.

The food started tasting better, the bed was fresher, and his clothes were cleaner. Now she was acting as hostess, like a real wife. She had taken Svanhild under her wing, and the two understood each other well. Einar suspected that Svanhild liked Holly more than she liked him. Since Agdis's death, Svanhild had mostly been raised by the kitchen servants, and whichever woman had time for her.

Einar had started detesting the idea of Holly leaving. If he could, he would make her stay forever. He enjoyed his life with her, and the fact that she would not die in childbirth was reassuring.

Einar followed Holly with his eyes as she came back to their table, which was in the center of the hall, and smiled at him. But there was an edge of tension in her expression. When she poured more mead into his cup and set the jug on the table, she sighed and said, "Solver just told me he enjoys the Orkneys and chasing the outlaws." She shook her head. "Also, the roast I made and the rolls I baked, apparently! He does not want to leave yet."

Einar studied her frown. Her eyes were dull with worry. Loki curse him. She was displeased that Solver was still here. She *wanted* to leave. She probably could not stop counting the days till she could go. Her sleeping with him must be just for fun. Her involvement in the household duties was probably just a way to pass the time. Her relationship with Svanhild must be just to enjoy the girl's company. The realization squeezed his gut till it hurt.

She would never stay.

His jaws worked, his gut tense with anger.

"Your rolls are good," he said without looking at her. "I am not surprised he wants to stay. But are you so eager to go?"

To all forest trolls, he should not have asked that. He should just keep his thoughts on the matter locked away.

She glanced at him, surprised, her eyebrows knit together. Her moss-colored eyes were so beautiful against her red hair in the cozy light of the oil lamps.

"Erm, well, yes, I needed to leave quite a while ago. I've been clear about that from the beginning. Why?" Her face softened and she swallowed. "Do you not want me to go?"

Einar breathed in deeply. Something in her question softened his anger and placed a burning hope in his chest.

"I never said that," he said, his voice rough. "I—did not think you staying was possible." He paused, his throat tensing. "Is it?"

Holly's mouth opened and closed as though she was trying to say something but could not manage. This was not a no. Maybe she would consider it?

But before she could answer, Svanhild came to Holly with her cat in her arms. Svanhild's eyes were bloodshot, her eyelids half closed, dark circles under her eyes, and her honey-colored hair in disarray.

"Why are you not asleep, Svanhild?" Einar asked. "You are clearly tired."

"Sleep does not come to me," she said.

She sat on the bench by Holly's side, the cat curled in her lap. Holly smiled warmly at her and rubbed her shoulder.

"Are you worried about something?" Holly asked.

"Thorir Treebeard is still somewhere around."

Einar's shoulders tightened. It was his fault his daughter had trouble falling asleep. Why had he not found the man yet? Holly exchanged a glance with him. She would be the one to reassure the girl. Not him.

"What if he takes you away, Holly?" Svanhild continued. "What if you leave us? I heard that you are from another time. A witch. Is this true?"

Einar tensed. "She is not a witch," he said.

That, he knew. The part about the future—he did not know if he quite believed that story himself. She looked Viking enough now, dressed like a local woman, in a long shift and an apron dress with brooches and threads of beads suspended between them; although, she often wore her strange jacket. But there were so many things that were different. Her way of cooking was unheard of. Her speech was strange at times. The clothes she had arrived in and her hairstyle were more a man's than a woman's. All that might mean she had told the truth about coming from another time, but he still did not quite believe it.

Holly bit her lip, a frown creasing the space between her eyebrows. She forced out a smile and took Svanhild's hands in both of hers.

"Look, your father is not going to let Thorir hurt you, me, or anyone else."

Einar breathed easier, Holly's support releasing the tension in his shoulders. She did behave like a true wife.

"And as for me...yes, I am from the future, but I'm not a witch."

She did not answer Svanhild's concern about leaving soon, and he understood why. She was Svanhild's new mother, and if she felt anything for the girl, she wouldn't want her to suffer another loss.

"How is the future?" Svanhild asked.

Holly smiled. "Well, it's a lot cleaner, at least where I live. I'm from Orlando, Florida. That's on the other side of the world. It's warm—we don't have winter—and there's always sun. But there are also big and dangerous beasts with giant jaws full of sharp teeth. They are called alligators and they live in the lakes. They can swim and move on the ground."

Svanhild gasped.

"Don't worry. They look scary, like a combination of a lizard and a dragon, but they won't harm you unless you want to harm them. Your father would totally kick a gator's ass," Holly said, and shot a quick smile at Einar, making his chest melt. He allowed a soft chuckle at Svanhild, who answered him with a smile.

"And how did you get to rule the big company you told me about?" Svanhild asked. "You must have a big army to conquer and protect it."

Einar shook his head slightly. This talk of a *company* and *business* that a woman could run was all very strange. So strange, he doubted Holly could have just made them up.

"No, sweetheart, I didn't use any force to get where I am, just my mind and hard work. I studied really hard at school and learned how to write and calculate. Then I went to university and worked my butt off there. Then I got an internship and made my way up the ladder."

"There are a lot of words I do not understand," Svanhild said. "But I would like to learn. I would like to read and write and calculate. I can already count."

"I'll teach you if you like," she said, "to write and speak English. That might come in handy in the future, especially here in the Orkneys, so close to kingdoms that speak English, or at least some version of it."

Svanhild nodded enthusiastically. Loki damn him, she was right. Holly was proving to be more useful than Einar wanted.

"And your family?" Svanhild said. "Do you have a mother and a father? Were you married before?"

He'd wondered about that himself but had not dared to ask, not wishing to feel more for her than he had wanted to.

"No," Holly said, and her voice shook. "I wasn't married, but I came close once. I wasn't lucky in love." She cleared her throat and shot a quick glance at Einar. "I suppose something about me was not right, or at least not what men want in a woman."

Einar could not believe his ears. What about her could seem wrong to any man? She was beautiful, strong, smart, and capable. If she was telling the truth, all those men from the future must be out of their minds. Not that he liked to think about any man in her life other than him.

"But yes, I do have parents," she said. "Although like you, sweetheart, I don't know the mother who gave birth to me.

Nor the father. My parents adopted me when I was a baby because they couldn't have children."

Svanhild petted Loki. "Now I have you, Holly," she said. "For me, you are like that mother that adopted you, aren't you?"

Holly's eyes watered and she gently stroked Svanhild's head. Einar exhaled. He was lucky she was so kind—another woman might not be gentle towards Svanhild. He did not even wish to imagine that.

"I suppose I am, in a way," she said.

Svanhild yawned and propped her head on her hand. "How did you travel in time, anyway?"

Holly exchanged a glance with Einar and smiled.

"I'll tell you, but then you go to bed, all right?"

"Yes, Holly."

"An old woman brought me to a place in Scotland, and there was a tree with a spindle carved on it. Then the spindle became golden and fell into my hands. The woman said I needed to help a Viking." She glanced at Einar. "So, I guess, here I am. Helping."

Einar fidgeted in his seat. He did not care that the more Holly told this story, the more believable it seemed. And if she was indeed from the future, the chances of her staying here were even less than if she was just a Pict.

"Was it a Norn?" Svanhild asked. "Golden spindles—Norns have them."

"I don't know," Holly said. "Maybe."

"Then, it is your destiny to be here. The Norn wants you here. With my father and me."

If it was true that a Norn had sent her here, Svanhild was right.

"I guess it is, at least for some time."

Einar's heart beat painfully against his ribs.

For some time.

Not forever.

"Okay, young lady, story time is over. It's bedtime now."

Svanhild nodded, her eyelids drooping. "Yes, Holly."

Holly kissed her on the cheek, and Svanhild went to her alcove, cuddling the cat in her arms.

Einar studied Holly as she took a sip of her mead. Was she indeed from the future? If she had been from Sutherland, he might have been able to persuade her to finish her business back home and return to him. There would have been hope.

But if she had traveled back in time, would she even consider staying?

"Do you like your life there? In the future?" Einar asked.

Holly glanced at him. "So, you believe me now?"

"Answer me, please."

Holly leaned back in her chair. "Yes, I like my life in the future. It's safe, and medicine is really advanced. Doctors—healers—can treat a lot of illnesses and do amazing surgeries. People live in comfort. There's plenty of food that you can buy in the stores all day long. Cars. Coffee. You can fly and be in another part of the world in a matter of hours. Women have the same rights as men and do important jobs. Like me—I run a billion-dollar company that desperately needs me back."

Einar listened with fascination. Some things didn't make sense to him. Flying? Food to be bought all day long? Advanced healers? It all sounded like the domain of the gods.

"Is that why you want to go back so much? The comfort?"

"Well, yes, of course. But also, my company was supposed to undergo a major merger, and I need to be there for that. I'm the head of the company. I've been working on this for three years. I haven't done anything but work for the last three years. No relationships. No traveling. I'm getting older, and I'm nowhere near having a family. So I just want to see the fruits of my hard work. If I don't oversee the merger, I'm afraid it might fail. Without me, they're probably freaking out. The police will be looking for me. My parents must be going insane. My friends..."

Einar nodded. She would never stay. That knowledge hurt.

"Besides, Thorir saw me. He's after me. I think that's why he stayed here."

Einar's teeth clenched hard. Yes, she must go. She would be safer in her time, without the threat of Thorir Treebeard finding her.

He gazed into his cup. The thought of her disappearing from his life very soon tore him apart. He needed to get used to being alone again. He needed to stop fooling himself and getting even more attached to Holly.

"Then I will make sure you can go as soon as possible," he said.

And because he could not look into her eyes any longer, because it hurt too much, he stood up and walked to the pasture where he would spend the night.

# CHAPTER THIRTEEN

May 30

Einar's eyes... His lips, warm and soft and hard at the same time on hers... His hard, hot, massive body gliding against her... His delicious weight on her... A shudder of excitement ran through Holly's body at the memories, her heart drumming. God, she missed Einar. He'd been searching for the outlaws for several days now, and she had barely seen him. His absence was like a dark hole, radiating dull emptiness within her.

Holly clapped her hands to shake off the thoughts—and the flour. She had just shown the cook how to make bread with yeast. When she'd been with Jack, she had thought he was the one. And she'd become more domestic and taken cooking and nutrition classes to get in shape for a pregnancy she'd thought Jack wanted with her. That was how she'd learned how to bake bread from scratch.

The Vikings only made flatbread, using yeast in mead and ale rather than bread. The flour was quite rough, not the fine powder Holly was used to. It needed to be ground with a millstone, and in order to get it fine enough, it had to be put through the stone several times. One of the thralls' jobs was to do that, although Holly had tried it, too, in order to help and also to know what it felt like.

Her arms had ached for a day afterwards.

She admired all of these strong women and men, doing manual labor all day long with no machines to help. They chopped firewood, scrubbed clothes in a nearby stream, ground flour, hauled water, produced cheese, and even wove or knitted cloth.

Holly wanted to help. These people did so much for her, and she felt that by churning butter, curing cheese, working in the garden, and doing other chores, she could repay that kindness.

Besides, it took her mind off Einar and how chilly he had been with her since the night Svanhild had asked her about the future. Ever since that talk, he had stopped sleeping in their bedroom and was avoiding her altogether. Yesterday, he had been away the whole day searching for Thorir, and the day before, he had been busy looking for more wood to store. The village was short on lumber because the wood that Einar had brought with them was gone now, and the Orkney Islands had very few trees.

Today—God knows where he was. Not in the main house.

It was for the best, Holly told herself. She was getting too attached to him. The sex blew her mind, but it was as though the whole world spun around him when he was in the room. As though he were her axis, and without him, everything would fall apart.

But she missed him. In her bones, she ached for him.

Through the sunlit entrance into the great hall, children shouted. One of the voices was Svanhild's, and something in her tone was off. She wiped her hands against a towel and hurried outside.

As Holly rounded the corner of the house, she saw Svanhild standing red-faced, her fists clenched, her eyebrows snapped together. By her feet laid a basket with flowers and plants scattered around the ground. Right next to her were two boys of the same age. One was a little taller, his hair like a nest of straw, and the other was shorter and dark haired. Holly recognized both. She had seen them from time to time in the village doing their chores.

"What's going on here?" Holly asked.

Svanhild looked down at her shoes. "Nothing."

One of the boys pursed his lips, the other frowned. Holly knew those looks. Construction and development was the world of men. And men sometimes talked about her—the young female boss—behind her back, especially the ones in entry-level positions. She'd walk into the employee lounge, and the caught-red-handed look on their faces would be both satisfactory and also a little painful. It reminded her of her big dark secret; that deep down, she was different from them. That she was defective to the degree that her real family had rejected her.

She also knew those men were just jealous of a woman taking what they thought they deserved.

The boys had the same look.

Holly's gut boiled with anger. They could talk all they wanted about her.

But not about Svanhild.

"Svanhild, did they do something to make you drop the basket?" Holly asked.

Svanhild shook her head without meeting Holly's eyes.

"What did they do?"

Svanhild kept silent, and Holly turned to the boys. "What did you two do to her?"

"If she says nothing, then it's nothing," the blond one said. "Maybe she's clumsy and dropped the basket."

Holly pressed her fists against her sides. "Tell me right now what you said to her, or I will curse you."

The boys' expressions went blank. "Curse?" the taller one said.

"Yes. I will curse you, and you will turn green like a troll, and no girl will ever want to marry you."

"You cannot curse us," the dark-haired boy said, but his voice rose as though he were asking a question.

"Oh, I can. And I will. I traveled in time to save your jarl and your village. Is this how you repay me? By lying?"

Her leather jacket was on because she was always cold here, coming from Florida, and she searched her pockets for some modern object to scare them off. She felt something hard.

"Aha!" she said, and their eyes widened in fear as she went into her inner pocket. She removed something plastic and pointed it at them like a sword. "Tell me the truth. What did the two of you do to Svanhild?"

They looked at the object in horror. Holly glanced at it, too, and saw that it was an unopened pregnancy test in a blue plastic wrapping. Her chest tightened at the thought that she'd probably never use it. When she had been going through the insemination procedures, she'd bought dozens of tests and had them everywhere with her. She'd used the tests at work, at home, even in restaurant bathrooms, wanting to know as soon as possible.

This was one last reminder.

Well, maybe it would scare the boys. "So?"

"I told her she was just a silly girl. That she does not know how to do anything except gather flowers and play with dolls.

We do all the work. She should be more grateful and do something for us."

Holly's anger burned her stomach. "Like what?" she said quietly. "What did you want her to do for you?"

The tall boy swallowed, his terrified eyes fixed on the pregnancy test. "Like give us a kiss for our hard work."

She felt Svanhild shrinking. Holly was just about to take the boys by their ears and drag them to their parents when a shadow fell over them.

"You wanted her to give you a kiss?" A voice thundered above her.

Einar.

If she had thought the boys were afraid of her, she had seen nothing yet. Their faces went as white as cotton, and they looked like they were about to drop dead on the ground.

Svanhild looked about the same.

Einar's expression was livid. His upper lip crawled back in a snarl, his eyebrows set in a straight line, and his nostrils flared. A vein beat in his temple.

"She is your chief's daughter!" he growled. "You dare lay one finger on her without her permission, you dare say one word that upsets her, and you will deal with me. She has no business answering to you. You must answer to her! If she wants you to wipe the floor with your arses, you do. If she wants you to walk on your hands, you do. If she wants to gather the flowers, then she gathers the flowers. I will teach you how to respect my daughter, my wife, and women in general. Come with me, you fools."

He took one giant step, grabbed them by the scruffs of their necks, and led them towards a house in the village. But he stopped for a moment and turned around. "Thank you for protecting her, Holly." His voice was still hard but softer now. "Svanhild, if anything like this happens again, you come to me, you hear me? Odin and Thor, you are growing up too fast."

He marched away quickly, leading the boys.

Holly breathed out and looked at Svanhild. The girl watched her father with an open mouth.

"Are you okay, honey?" Holly asked.

Svanhild finally glanced back at her and nodded. "Yes." She sank to her knees and began putting the flowers and herbs into the basket. Holly bent down to help her. "I did nothing, you know," Svanhild said. "I went to pick healing herbs because Bera asked me to."

"Oh, I know you're not lazy, honey. You don't need to justify yourself to me. They are idiots."

"Maybe. But I did not want to tell on them. I knew they were unfair, but I did not know what to say so that they would leave me alone. I do not know what is wrong with me."

Holly stopped Svanhild and made her look at her. "There's absolutely nothing wrong with you, Svanhild. Your father is right. You are the chief's daughter. And soon, you'll be the jarl's daughter. You'll have all the say in the world. If anyone wants to hurt you or do anything against your will, you tell them you'll have your father and his men come and cut their ears off. Or whatever you Vikings do to your enemies."

Svanhild smiled, and her back straightened. "Right."

"Yes, right," Holly said. "Do not forget who you are. Your father will turn the world upside down before he lets anything happen to you."

Svanhild leaned forward and hugged Holly. "Thank you. If my mother was alive, she would have told me what to say to bullies. My father just scowls at me. How am I supposed to know all this?"

Holly pressed the girl to her and kissed the crown of her head. She wished her mom would have had a similar pep talk with her instead of constantly looking for what Holly had done wrong.

"He just doesn't know how to talk to you, hon. He loves you very much, even if he doesn't know how to show it."

Svanhild bent down again and continued to gather the herbs. "Maybe. But I know the gods gave me you. You are my new mother, and you will teach me everything I have missed."

Holly forced out a smile, but inside, the pain of guilt stabbed at her. Because if even Einar didn't care if she left or stayed, she knew it wasn't only her heart that would break when she left.

# CHAPTER FOURTEEN

June 1

It was a quiet evening. The sun hung like a red dragon's eye between pink-and-orange clouds. The sea was almost still, and Einar inhaled fresh air. Next to him sat his wife, her skin golden in the sunset, her eyes luminous. He had seen her descending the small hill to the cliff and followed to make sure she was safe. She had sat down without a word and stared at the sunset, and he had sat down by her side. Far below, the sea caressed the white sand, and he longed to touch her as gently.

"Thank you, Holly," Einar said. "What you did for Svanhild... I should have protected her. I should have been there."

"She's a good girl." Holly smiled. "Those jerks needed to be taught a lesson. You've done much better than me."

"And yet, you protected my child. You are a strong woman. A she-wolf."

Holly studied him and giggled. "A she-wolf? Me? My

mother would have found at least twenty things wrong in that statement. And this time, I'd agree with her."

"And I would make sure your mother never got a say in anything concerning you again. She does not sound like she has a truthful opinion of you."

"She's my harshest critic." Holly sighed. "I wonder how my biological mother was. I guess that is why I came to Scotland and started all that research. Because I never felt that I was okay. Deep down, I feel like there's some sort of flaw that's impossible to get rid of, and that's why I don't have my biological parents. Like, they had to get rid of me." She pressed her lips together and looked down. "And other things."

"If you think so, you must be insane. Everything you have touched since your arrival has made life here better. Made my life better."

Holly glanced at him, surprised. Then an expression of loss crossed her face. He wanted to brush a fingertip across her forehead and wipe those creases away. Make her smile again.

"I'm just repaying my debt, Einar. I can't just sit on my ass and get served dinner. But if you want my professional opinion, your personnel could work much more efficiently."

Einar raised his eyebrows and chuckled. "What?"

"Your servants could work and accomplish more in less time."

"How so?"

"Well, you have several people working the kitchens, and right now, everyone is doing everything. But if you made a sort of conveyor, it would go faster. Like, one person is only on peeling duty, the next one on chopping, the third one on meat cutting. And you could use the same principle for everything else. Planting. Harvesting. Weaving."

At first, Einar thought that it was the strangest thing he'd ever heard, but when he imagined it, he realized how much faster things would go.

"To all gods, you are right," he said. "Is that one of your futuristic ideas?"

"Yes." Holly smiled, clearly pleased with his compliment. "Also, you could build a chimney."

"A chimney?"

"Yes. Right now, your firepits just smoke up the whole hall. The tiny hole in the roof only lets a little smoke out. A chimney is a high sort of tower above the firepit. It funnels the smoke directly from the firepit out through the roof. It's safe, and there would be much less smoke in the room."

Einar gazed at her with wonder. "You must teach my men how to do that before you leave."

A fleeting expression of sadness crossed her face when he said the last word. "Sure, Einar."

He did not want to think of the moment she'd leave him. "What else can you recommend?"

"Well, you have a problem with few trees here, but you still need fire. I've heard Ireland is rich with turf or peat. Do you know what that is?"

Einar felt the muscles of his face fall. Why had he not thought of this himself?

"I know very well what it is. In Norway, we use turf from swamps. I must send men to look for it on the islands. Your advice, your help...have meant more than gold to me. I wish—" he cut himself off as her eyes burned and lit up with hope.

"You wish what?" Holly asked.

He wished she never had to leave.

"I wish I'd never stopped kissing you," he said, pulling her close. The need for her, hot and greedy, sucked in his gut. He covered her mouth with his, and she met him with a heat and desire that mirrored his own.

Tomorrow, Solver would sail off. That was what he had told Einar today. Einar's heart had sunk at the news because he only had days left with Holly, and he needed her more than a ship needed water now.

"I have been a fool to stay away from you," he whispered against her lips. "I should have taken every opportunity to be with you."

Holly frowned. Not now! He was so happy swimming in her delicious scent, drinking the sweet mead of desire from her lips.

"Why?" she asked.

Loki's stinky armpits. He'd hoped to make love to her first, and then give her the news.

"Solver is leaving tomorrow," he said, letting her slide gently onto the grass.

Her eyes widened a little, and she looked out over the sea. "Oh," she said.

Still, she did not move. "Are you not in a hurry to gather your things and be ready to leave at the first opportunity?" he asked.

She shook her head as though to shake off a dream. "I don't know how to say goodbye to Svanhild."

Yes, his poor daughter would be devastated. Holly would have been a wonderful mother to her. Another stab at his heart.

"You'll need to talk to her," Holly said. "Support her. She doesn't have anyone to talk to."

It was true, and she pushed right into his pain points. "Woman," he said as he pulled her closer. "I do not have talking in mind at all right now."

He kissed her again, deeper this time. He needed her. He hungered for her. His tongue parted her lips, sinking into her, and was greeted by her playful tongue. She teased him and nipped at him and turned the kindling desire in his blood into a raging wildfire.

"I want you, Holly," he growled. "Can you feel how much I want you?"

He lifted her up and sat her on his lap so that her sex was pressed against his. She circled her pelvis, sending a wave of hot pleasure through him as her movement caressed his cock. He gave out a long moan.

"Mmmmmmmm." He heard the sound leave his throat.

"You like that, don't you?" she said, then looked back at the village. They were a safe enough distance away that someone would need to deliberately come and look for them before they'd see them. But Einar refused to allow anyone to see his wife naked. Her body was for him alone.

"I must have you now," he said.

"Naughty." Holly smiled. "I like naughty."

He grinned and lowered his head to her breasts. He cupped one in each of his hands and massaged them slightly, then took one nipple in his mouth and sucked through two layers of fabric, wetting her dress.

"Oh God, this is so hot..." she moaned, her head rolling back.

He continued his game, sucking and circling his tongue, biting her nipple slightly, then sucking harder. She moaned and groaned the most arousing sounds, and he repeated the process with the second breast. Then she put her hands in his hair, every touch spilling smooth pleasure through his veins.

With one hand, he slowly reached up her leg—her long, sculpted leg that he adored—and covered her sex with his palm. Gently, he spread her folds, making her gasp, and found the sweetest spot in her body. She gulped for air, her fingers digging into his back. He circled the hard button, and Holly ground her hips against him and wiggled from pleasure. With another finger, he dipped into her hot depths and noted with satisfaction that she was soaking wet.

He undid his trousers and removed his throbbing cock. "You are so ready for me," he said.

"Oh yes," Holly moaned.

She rose a little and let him place his erection against her entrance. Looking into her green eyes, he entered her, so sweet and tight. She gasped, her body tensing in pleasure, and then she began riding him. He sank in the depths of her eyes as he thrust upwards, meeting her hips.

They were perfect—her tightness around him, the soft roundness of her breasts, her body so willing to take him. And he was more than happy to give.

He'd give her anything she wanted every day of his life.

He sped up, the four nights without her making his cock hungrier than ever for her. She sped up, too, her moans like pleas now, and she was tight and hot around him.

Soon, he recognized the sweet, high-pitched sounds she always made before she found her release, and he knew he would come with her. He needed to be careful and pull out.

One thrust.

Two.

Three...

"Ahhhh," she cried, as her muscles convulsed around him, and his own release began covering him like a giant wave.

He needed to pull out... Just a moment more. He still had time... But his body shuddered violently as he held on to her, and she to him.

And he spilled his seed in her again.

He hated losing control. But, gods, how good it felt to have her convulse around him as he rocked on the waves of his own pleasure.

He would be angry with himself later. He already felt the dark tension of that anger growing somewhere deep.

But now, just for this moment, he pushed it away.

And as they swayed together in each other's arms like branches of a tree on a slight breeze, Einar whispered, "I wish you could stay."

He hoped she had not heard him, but his heart ached as she whispered back, "Me too."

# CHAPTER FIFTEEN

June 2

The pier was full of people. The wind blew hard gusts against Holly's face, bringing relief from the nausea that had been bothering her on and off since last night. Must have been the grilled herring. She hadn't wanted to eat it. It had smelled too fishy and wasn't the freshest catch. But she had to eat something, and it had been either grilled herring or skyr for dinner. She hated the pungent Norse yogurt.

She inhaled the freshness of the chilly air and instantly felt better. She needed to maintain her composure, look like the perfect chieftain's wife. This would be the last time she'd have to do it, because, at the end of the pier, Solver's men threw sacks and chests with food, personal belongings, and Einar's tribute to King Harald into a ship.

Solver was finally leaving.

Einar stood next to Holly as Solver looked inside his belt purses for something while mumbling words of wisdom to

Einar. Einar looked like he could not care less about any words that Solver had to say. His eyebrows were snapped together, his eyes dark. He was as gloomy and temperamental as the gray sky that hung above them. He clenched and unclenched his fists, and Holly placed one hand on him, noting that his skin was cold for the first time since she'd met him.

He shot a quick glance at her and inhaled deeply, then let out the air, his face relaxing a little.

"There," Solver said. "Found it."

He held out a necklace with a pendant to Holly, and she took it, studying the thick silver chain and the Mjölnir. This was clearly men's jewelry.

"Is this yours?" she asked.

"It was. But I have one from the king. Take it. For luck. A time traveler who has married a Viking jarl." He chuckled. "You will need Thor's protection, especially with Thorir still around."

Holly smiled. "Are you sure?"

"Yes, mistress. I need to be on the jarl of Orkney's wife's good side. Besides, I want to thank you for the rolls and other excellent cooking."

"Thank you so much, Solver." She wanted to hug the man, his young, good-humored face watching her with kindness. He gave a small bow, then squatted level with Svanhild, who stood by Holly's side.

"Keep an eye on your father," he said. "He needs you. Here," he added and placed something in her hand—an ancient, thick, uneven silver coin. "This is from the Iberian Peninsula. I obtained it in a profitable trading mission. It is for you to taste adventure. Maybe one day, you will see the peninsula for yourself."

"Enough, Solver," Einar said. "The only adventures she will have will be safe ones."

Svanhild's eyes burned. "Thank you. May Odin bless you on your journey."

Next, Solver came to Einar and stood before him. He was shorter than Einar, but still much taller than Holly. Everyone was shorter than Einar.

Solver clasped Einar's shoulders with both his hands. "I wish you luck, Einar, jarl of Orkney. You will need it. Get that bastard Thorir. I am sorry I must go and cannot help you catch him, but Harald is expecting me, and I do not want to give him reason to come here personally. This woman by your side is a good thing. May Freyja and Frigg bless you with many, many children. I will tell Harald his wish in the Orkneys was fulfilled."

Holly could almost hear Einar's teeth grind. The two men took each other in a bear hug, clapping each other roughly on the back. Then Solver stepped away.

His ship was now loaded and ready. He said, "I will tell a fine poem about the jarl of Orkney and his wife."

"Let Ran and Aegir give you a smooth sail," Einar said as Solver walked towards the ship.

Holly's heart squeezed. It was hard to say goodbye to Solver. It meant she'd soon say goodbye to everyone here. To Svanhild.

To Einar.

Why did the thought hurt as though a concrete wall crushed her?

Soon, the ship was far away, and people returned to the village. Guards threw careful glances around them.

"I would take you to Scotland myself," Einar said in a surprisingly soft, almost sad voice that made Holly's stomach tense painfully, "but with Thorir lurking around, I cannot leave the people. It would be safest for you to leave as soon as possible, though. The boat will be ready in three days. You will have your wish fulfilled."

"Three days?" she said. But what she wanted to say was, *so soon*?

"Three days," he confirmed, and walked faster towards the house.

People liked Solver here. He was good entertainment, so Einar supposed it was not surprising that many went around with sad faces for the rest of the day.

Einar and Holly were passing through the main hall, which was now quiet and dark as people were getting ready to sleep. The smell of dinner still lingered in the air.

"Holly!" Svanhild called from her alcove. Einar stopped, and Holly did, too, looking in Svanhild's direction. Something hurt in him as he realized that even though he was Svanhild's father, she never called for him.

Holly gripped Einar's hand and led him towards the alcove. Svanhild held her blanket to her chin, looking worried.

"Yes, honey?" Holly said. "Everything all right?"

Svanhild sat up. "Forgive me, Father, I just wanted Holly."

That hurt even more, like a hand twisting his heart. But he was at fault, no one else. He gave a short nod and turned, but Holly stopped him and made him turn back to Svanhild.

"Wait, maybe your father can help, too. What is it?"

Svanhild looked at her hands. "I wanted to ask if you could stay with me until I fall asleep. The outlaws are out there, and Solver left, and I am sad."

Einar's heart was crushed. His poor daughter. He should be much better at protecting her.

"Of course, we will stay until you fall asleep, won't we, Einar?"

Einar frowned. Never in his life had he put his daughter to sleep. His wife had never showed him how, and he felt like a giant, clumsy bear next to a mouse.

"No, I better leave you to it," he said.

"No, you better stay. Svanhild wants you to stay, don't you, sweetheart?"

Svanhild pressed out a smile. "Yes, Father, I just did not think you would like to. But of course I want you to stay. It is even better with you. You have the ax."

Holly chuckled, and Einar could not help but smile, too. He nodded, and he and Holly settled on the floor by the alcove.

"Lie down, dear," Holly said. "Your father will tell you a good-night story."

"A what?" Einar asked, alarmed.

"A story. You guys have so many. All those myths and legends of Thor, Loki, Freyja, and all the others. Just pick one that would calm her and tell it. Would you like that, Svanhild?"

She nodded enthusiastically. "Oh yes. One about Loki."

Einar scratched his head. He had never told a story before, only listened to them. This would be awkward, and Svanhild would hate him for it. He was not a good skald. Where was Solver when one needed him?

He sighed. He supposed a story he always enjoyed was how Loki made the mighty god Thor dress as a woman and marry a giant.

"One day, Mjölnir, Thor's hammer, disappeared," he began nervously. "Thor was a powerful warrior, but he did not know what to do. He needed someone smart. So when Thor discovered that his hammer was missing, he went to Loki."

"Loki," Svanhild whispered and cuddled the cat that Einar now noticed was sticking just his nose out from under the furs.

Holly smiled at Einar and squeezed his hand.

"Loki asked Freyja for the feather cloak that allowed her to fly. With it, he flew to the lands of giants and found out what had happened. The lord of the giants, Thrym, had stolen the hammer and refused to give it back.

"'What will it take?' Loki asked. He knew there was no such thing as a no.

"'Freyja,' the giant said. 'I want to marry her, the goddess of beauty and love.'"

Svanhild gasped, and Einar hid a smile. By some miracle, he found joy in telling the story. His voice softened, and he could even speak with different voices.

"So Loki returned to Asgard with the news, and sure enough, Freyja said no.

"But Loki knew there was no such thing as no. The gods of Asgard held a council, and it was suggested that Thor should disguise himself as Freyja and wear the bridal dress.

"'I like it!' Loki said. 'And I will dress as your maiden. We will retrieve Mjölnir and kill the giant who took it.'

"'No,' Thor said. 'I will not dress as a woman. This is unmanly.'"

Svanhild giggled. "Loki is so clever." She petted her kitten. It was the first time in Einar's life that Svanhild had smiled or laughed for him. Something in his chest melted.

"But of course Loki knew there was no such thing as no, and soon he and Thor both dressed as women and went to Thrym's longhouse.

"'Are you ill, goddess?' Thrym said. 'You are hiding behind a veil, and your eyebrows are so bushy... Is it a beard I see?'

"'It is only a disguise to hide her from harm on the way here,' Loki said.

"'I should like to begin the wedding,' Thor said, making his voice as high-pitched as possible. 'Bring Mjölnir to bless the ceremony.'

"'As you wish, my love,' said Thrym.

"Then the hammer was brought by twenty giants. So many were needed to carry it, while Thor could swing it with just one arm.

"And as his precious hammer lay by his feet, he leaned down and took it, the feeling sweet and familiar.

"'This will show you how to steal my hammer!' he cried. He took off his veil and struck the giant right in his ugly face.

"He swung again and killed ten more giants. Another swing, and the rest of them lay dead.

"Thor straightened and sighed happily. Then he pointed Mjölnir at Loki, who was looking around with a proud smirk.

"'And you, never again make me dress as a woman.'

"But truth be told, even such a mighty warrior as Thor sometimes needs a bit of Loki."

Svanhild sighed, a happy smile spread on her face, her eyes drifting closed. "Thank you, Father. I loved that story."

He smiled back at her. He and Holly stood up, and he had just turned to go when Holly nudged him. "Kiss her," she whispered.

"What?"

"Give her a good-night kiss."

Einar swallowed. Why was he so rigid and hesitant to show his daughter how much he loved her? But something had changed today, as though the ice had been broken. He took a step to the alcove, leaned down, and kissed his daughter's head for the first time in eight years. She smelled of lavender, childhood, and something innocent and dear. Something he thought he had lost. But there it was. He had found it again like Thor found his hammer.

He brushed her head once, and her breathing deepened with a sigh before her face softened in sleep.

Einar and Holly quietly walked to his bedchamber. And his

heart ached and stretched, feeling as if it just grown to the size of Midgard.

# CHAPTER SIXTEEN

JUNE 4

THE PREGNANCY TEST in Holly's hand shook as she stared at the white window that would show her in one to two minutes if her life would change forever. The day was sunny and bright but still cold. She shivered and huddled into her leather jacket. She was behind the corner of the main house. She couldn't wait in the outhouse, and she wanted some privacy.

Holly's nausea hadn't gone away. Her stomach turned from pretty much any food except for bread. Her nipples had started to ache, and her breasts swelled slightly. She had cramps, but she always got them before her period. And yet, it didn't come. She wasn't regular, which was one of the reasons she couldn't conceive a baby. Through the years, she'd read every article, every forum post, and every book on pregnancy.

And she knew cramps were one of the signs.

Her breath came out in a shudder, her feet icy cold. The one "test" line appeared, which meant the test worked fine. Now the question was, would the second vertical line appear, too, to form a plus.

She couldn't watch. She couldn't wait anymore. Her whole body tensed and shook. She closed her eyes and slid down the wall to sit on the sun-warmed grass. Sucking in air, she exhaled shakily.

What if she was pregnant? Would that change the fact that she was leaving tomorrow? How would Einar react? He didn't want any more children, so he would probably freak out.

Was she ready to see the result? Had a minute passed? It felt like an eternity.

She opened her eyes.

A pale-blue line crossed the first one.

A plus.

Holly gasped and dropped the test to the grass. With trembling fingers, she picked it up. Her eyes burned and blurred, and she wiped them, wanting to make sure she hadn't hallucinated. She looked closer, then held the test farther away, then turned it so that she could see it in the light of the sun.

It was there, the plus. It didn't disappear.

She put her hand on her lower belly, tears falling from her eyes, a smile spreading from ear to ear.

She was not alone anymore. She was pregnant.

Her chest expanded as though a balloon were inflating inside of her lungs. Her heart danced, and her whole body felt as though it were about to float into the sky and fly away.

Einar might not want more children, but she needed to tell him anyway. Maybe he'd change his mind.

She ran. She needed to tell Einar. How ironic was it that no amount of medicine could do this for her in Orlando, and yet here, all it had taken was that first time with a Viking.

She knew he was on guard today, on the other side of the village.

"Einar!" she cried. "Einar!"

He appeared from behind one of the houses immediately, his giant frame launching at her without hesitation, his eyes looking for the source of threat.

"Did you see him? Where?" he cried, one hand removing the ax from his belt.

She ran into his arms and buried her face in his chest, her tears soaking into his white linen tunic. He hugged her with one arm, the other still holding the ax.

"What is it? Who did this to you?"

He let go of her and pulled her chin up.

"Who dared? Tell me. I will cut his balls off."

She shook her head. "No one. I just..." She sniffed. "My whole life, I believed there was something wrong with me. That I'm defective. My real parents didn't want me and left me for adoption. My mother has always found things I could do better. And men...every single one broke up with me."

His eyes softened, and the sun caught in his hair, bringing out strands of dark gold and copper.

"What are you saying? Those men are complete fools. Had I had you..." He broke off and looked down. "Were you not due to leave tomorrow, I would never let you go."

She blinked, her heart aching, body melting, tears crawling. "What are you saying?"

"I confess, Holly. I could not breathe for the last two days. The thought of you leaving me forever—it is as though Odin pierces me through the heart with his spear." He exhaled sharply. "I want you to stay. Be my wife. Everything is better with you here. Svanhild is happier." He swallowed. "I am happier. I could not wish for a better wife than you. I want to build Orkney together with you."

It was as though he were breathing life into her. Her head

spun, her stomach filling with lightness, bubbles of joy tickling her heart.

Could she consider staying? Could she really abandon her life back in Orlando? Her parents? Her employees? Her friends?

And what about the fact that a psycho was somewhere around the island, hunting her, wanting to murder her in the name of Odin? It would not just be her who'd die, but also her baby. Back in Orlando, no one wanted her dead.

And still, her heart whispered that she would love to stay, be Einar's wife, raise two children with him—Svanhild and this baby.

She cupped his jaw. "I think I would stay, Einar."

He dropped the ax and hugged her and whirled her around him, burying his face in her hair. Then he gently set her on the ground. "I swear, that troll's shit Thorir will not disturb a hair on your head." He touched his Mjölnir pendant.

"But there's more," she said. Oh God, she was about to tell the father of her child that she was pregnant. She knew Einar wouldn't be thrilled, but he wanted her to stay. Surely, he'd be fine with that. He was a kind man. He'd never break up with her over her pregnancy.

"What is it?"

She removed the pregnancy test from her pocket, checking that the plus was still there. It was. She turned it to face Einar.

"What does this rune mean?" he asked.

"That I'm pregnant," she breathed out.

The smile faded from his lips, slowly replaced by confusion, and then anger. Fury. And an edge of fear.

"What?" he barked.

"This is a pregnancy test. I had it with me from my time. I just checked, and it shows that I'm pregnant."

He took a step back. His face was ashen, his upper lip crawled up.

"No," he said.

"Yes."

"How can you be with child? This is not my child, then."

"Of course it is. I haven't had sex with anyone but you."

"But we married only two sennights ago. You need moons to know..."

"No, this is an early prediction test. It shows—"

Einar roared, his hands curled into fists, his eyes dark and haunted, something terrifying lurking in their depths.

"No. You cannot do this to me," he said. "You said you cannot have children."

"I was wrong," she whispered. "All it took was you. It's a miracle, Einar."

He shook his head, his eyes wild, looking like a cornered animal. Holly's world was falling apart, the lightness, the happiness, the warmth gone. Her body hurt all over.

"But I do not want any more children. I do not want a wife who wants them. I lost the love of my life in childbirth, and I swore long ago I would never endure that again. I thought you were perfect. You said you could not get pregnant, but I still did not want to risk it by spilling my seed in you. And now this..." He ran his fingers through his hair. "I cannot endure it if you die giving birth to this child."

Holly shook all over, but this time, it was not nervousness. It was world-shattering pain.

Finally, the one man who mattered the most in her life, who had just said she was perfect, had found a flaw.

And that flaw was the best thing that had ever happened to her.

Einar picked up his ax and shook his head. "You have just opened the gates to Helheim for me."

Without another word, he left. And she bled and ached inside. She had been wrong. The glimpse of happiness she'd had with Einar had been an illusion. And she was back to being left, to being unwanted.

Except now, she was not alone. She had a baby to protect, and the safest place for her child would be in her own time, away from Thorir and all the other dangers of the Viking world.

# CHAPTER SEVENTEEN

Later that evening, Einar was on his way home with his hands full of hare and his heart full of pain. He had gone out after his talk with Holly, in desperate need of a distraction from the thing he had been afraid most in the world.

That, he would meet a woman he cared for. And that, again, she would risk dying because he impregnated her.

He did not want to think about Agdis or Holly, but as he'd set the traps and waited for game, his mind had raced back, plucking the most painful memories like the ripest strawberries in the forest.

He'd remembered the joy of holding Svanhild for the first time, and the scare he got while Agdis was in labor. He remembered how, during the second labor, her pains had been much stronger—so strong, the whole village must have heard her. Despite the midwife's protests, he had rushed into their bedchamber. There was nothing that would scare him more than waiting on the other side of the door, not knowing, fighting an invisible enemy he had no power over—fate.

He'd held Agdis's hand and wiped her forehead with a cool, damp cloth.

"The babe is too big," the midwife said. "It will never pass."

The meaning of her words fell on him like a giant tree, crushing him so that every muscle, every limb hurt with the agony of a thousand deaths.

If he could, he would die for her. He would take the burden, the pain, the desperation of being trapped in a body that could not do what it was supposed to do.

But all he could do was be with her, listen to her mindless screams, and wait until she died.

And then when she was finally gone, he had to go out of the room, his body numb, his world dark, and look at the two-winter-old Svanhild.

"Mama," she said and chewed on the wooden doll he had carved for her earlier that year. "Mama?"

Even though she was so little, he could swear, she understood that she would never see her mother again. He saw something in her eyes dim, and she cried.

And he had walked away. He could not look her in the eyes. She needed her mother. She did not need him. She would never need him.

There was no way in the world he could endure this again with Holly or let Svanhild go through it again. That would be the end of him.

It would be better for Holly to go. Return to her time. Based on what she had said, the healers could help her. She and the babe would be alive. He would rather know she was alive and well somewhere else, with his child, than have her stay with him under the danger of childbirth, something he could not shield her from.

The sun was already setting when he approached the darkening village.

"Einar!" Lofarr cried. He stood guard on the edge of the village. "Finally, you came back. We did not know where you were."

"What is it?" Einar's reverie fled, battle fury and fear filling him. "Thorir?"

"We found where they are hiding. There is a cave on the other side of the island. They were out fishing, but they will return now, and we can ambush them."

"At last, good news," Einar said. "Let us saddle up the horses and end those bastards."

HOLLY WATCHED Svanhild doing some sort of crochet or knitting with one needle. The main hall was quiet, the servants cleaning the kitchen, sweeping the floor, and putting clean dishes and utensils in their places. The sight of the household being put in order, and of Svanhild's hands moving in a repetitive manner, calmed her, and somehow soothed the pain that radiated all over her body.

This was her last night with the girl who had become like a daughter to her, her last night with Einar. Her last night in the place that accepted her so warmheartedly. In the place where, for the first time in her life, she felt like she was part of a family.

Holly thought about the first time she had seen Einar, how he'd saved her from Thorir. Their wedding, the hot kiss that had made her burn and swell. Svanhild, how much Holly loved this smart, lovely, kind girl.

How she treasured it all.

She was going to miss them so much. Back home, she would have to raise her baby alone. Her parents would help, of course, but she'd never have this feeling of a complete family—

husband and children. All she'd have would be her work and her baby.

"Look, Holly, this is not difficult. It is *nålbinding*, needle-binding." The needle in her hand was thick and large, made of some sort of bone or ivory, and her hands worked fast. "You wrap the yarn around your thumb, pass the needle through the loop and form a new one, but do not tighten. Then pass the needle through the new loop. This is how this chain forms."

"Oh, sweetie, you are so good at this. What are you making?"

"Mittens for Father, for winter. Then I will make socks. And a hat for when he goes out hunting."

Holly smiled, but tears filled her eyes. For when he goes out hunting... She'd never see him hunt in winter. He was out now, chasing Thorir. Finally, they had found the psycho's hideout. Well, at least if they caught Thorir, she'd know that Svanhild would not be in as much danger.

Einar had left a few guards, just in case, but almost every man had gone. They'd wanted to finish this once and for all.

Holly swallowed the lump in her throat. "He will be very h—"

The doors flew open, and female screams cut through the air. Men stood in the doorframe, their figures tall, faces dirty, beards disheveled, axes and swords bloody.

Thorir.

Holly jumped to her feet, shielding Svanhild. Her body felt as heavy as lead and as cold as an ice statue.

"Give me the needle, Svanhild," Holly said quietly, her hand behind her back. The girl placed the needle in Holly's hand. Holly didn't have just herself but also her baby and Svanhild to protect.

Thorir pinned her with his predator eyes. "There you are,

witch." He moved towards her, his ax in his hand. "Finally, Odin will have his sacrifice."

# CHAPTER EIGHTEEN

EINAR and his men hid in the bushes on top of the cliffs for a long while. Every time black waves crashed against the white sand far below, but no one appeared, the worry coiled in the pit of Einar's stomach grew. When the moon was high in the starlit sky, and still nothing moved on the shore, Einar knew Thorir and his men would not come tonight.

Which meant...

"Thor strike me with his hammer," Einar spat and jumped up. "The village! They are raiding the village."

His men echoed with angry, worried shouts and darted for their horses. They were on the opposite side of the island. They would never get there in time, but they had to try.

*Fool. Fool. Fool,* the hooves of his horse thumped against the ground.

He had been tricked so easily. As though he were not a grown man, a leader tempered in battles, but a boy. A naive, foolish boy who was about to lose everything and everyone dear to him.

Svanhild, his only child. Holly, the woman his heart ached

for, the woman his body demanded, the woman who nourished his soul.

And another babe, the unborn babe.

"Hya!" Einar yelled, digging his heels into the horse's sides. "Come on, you beast!"

His unborn babe.

Would that be a son? Holly had said he would have three sons...

His eyes grew damp. Rain? No, the sky was clear.

Tears. He clenched his teeth so hard he thought he felt them crunch. Helplessness, desperation, fury, all roared within him, turning his muscles to stone, something hot and painful swirling in his gut. He should have sent Holly away today.

Could the dozen men he'd left behind protect everyone? If Thorir harmed anyone, Einar would consider blood eagling the man a mercy.

The village was quiet, the thatched roofs and the stone houses silver in the moonlight. A barely noticeable tang of blood hung in the air. Near the first houses, two of his men lay dead. They found the rest of the men lying dead around the village, signs of battle on them. In the streets, hay, shattered jars, spilled grain, broken eggs, and torn pieces of cloth were scattered among the buildings. Thorir's men had raided, all right. And they were already gone.

His ax and shield ready, Einar ran towards his house, limbs stiff with fear.

Inside were women—the kitchen servants and house thralls—with knives and pitchforks ready. One lay in an alcove with her head bandaged. The house looked like a storm had hit—tables and benches overturned, food and utensils thrown around, the scent of spilled mead in the air.

No Svanhild.

No Holly.

The ground sank under his feet as though giants had cleaved open the floor, and he was falling into the abyss of despair.

Thorir had his girls—his pregnant wife and his only daughter.

"They were alive when he took them," Bera said. "He asked me to tell you that you can come with gold as ransom for Svanhild."

His hands shook. "And my wife?"

Bera looked down. "He said not to come for her, Jarl."

He was looking into the abyss, dark and endless, and eternal. The madness that was waiting for him if he lost everyone he loved in this world.

He turned to his men. "Ship. Now. *Now*. We do not come back until we find them, dead or alive."

His men nodded, somber.

"And until I send Thorir to Helheim."

# CHAPTER NINETEEN

THEY SAILED FOR A LONG TIME, the wind flapping in the sails of Einar's longship, which Thorir had stolen. Holly huddled with Svanhild by the mast, in the fur cloak they had been allowed to bring. Even in June, it was cold on the bare sea.

"It will be all right," Holly whispered to Svanhild, not really believing the words herself. "Your father will come. He'll save us."

She glanced back at Thorir, whose eyes always bored into her.

"Do you hear, Thorir," she shouted with spite. "He'll come to save us."

She expected him to rush towards her and hit her, like he had in the tent. But he continued staring at her, lazily. "I hope so," he said.

The men who rowed on both sides of the ship threw heavy, solemn glances at her. She shut up. There was absolutely nothing she could do to free them right now. She still had Svanhild's needle, though, and knew the moment to use it would come.

It was morning when they arrived. The island looked like any other Orkney Island. There was a large farm, a village almost, with round stone buildings scattered around the green hills. Cows and sheep were on the pastures higher up. But since they had sailed the whole night, could these still be the Orkneys? They must be somewhere else. Was this part of the Shetland Islands, farther north?

Men and a few women walked around the settlement, their faces stern, their clothes ragged. They glanced at Thorir with barely hidden fear and avoided direct eye contact. What would happen if Einar didn't find Holly and Svanhild in time? Holly shuddered at the thought.

Holly and Svanhild were locked in a stone shed. There were no windows, just hay scattered around. It smelled like earth and animals.

She'd kill Thorir before she let him do anything to Svanhild or to her. She'd put the needle through his eye...or maybe his throat.

She shuddered again. Was she planning a murder? But a mother did anything to save her children.

Anything.

And now that she had the most precious gift of all, the little baby inside of her, she wouldn't let anyone harm it as long as she had any strength left in her.

Svanhild and Holly banged on the door and cried for help, but of course nothing happened. They spent the first day alone. They checked the door and every corner but didn't find a way out. To distract the girl from their situation, Holly told Svanhild more about the future: about airplanes, cars, TV, movies, and music. Svanhild told Holly stories about Einar and their life with her uncle Rögnvald. She told her about the cousins who were her friends, how she had found Loki, hurt and abandoned in the forest, and nursed him back to health, and how Uncle Rögnvald had taught her the game *hnefatafl*.

Then Holly lost track of time. By the end of the first day, the lamp they had been given ran out of oil, but soon, a woman brought them another lamp as well as food and water. After that, she came once a day to bring more supplies and to empty their night pots. Holly tried to talk to her, but she kept her mouth shut, clearly afraid. She moved hastily and hurried back outside as soon as she could.

It must have been the fifth day when Holly heard heavy steps outside the door, not the usual light steps of the servant woman. Holly and Svanhild sat straight up, and Holly's fingers tightened around the needle she had pinned under her apron dress. Someone removed the bar, the door opened, and a warrior stood in the doorframe.

He entered and put bowls of food and a jar of water on the floor.

Then he turned towards Holly. She backed away instinctively, but his strong hand grasped her upper arm and yanked her up. Svanhild jumped up, too, her expression terrified.

"You come with me. Thorir wants you," the warrior said.

"I'll be back, Svanhild," Holly said over her shoulder as the man dragged her outside. "Don't you dare touch her, you hear me?"

The man only grunted. Outside, she looked around frantically for help, but no one even paid attention to her. It was as though she were a goat or a sheep being dragged away. No doubt, they were probably used to slaves. Maybe these people were all slaves.

"What does he want with me?" she asked, trying to free her arm. "Let me go. Help us escape. I'll tell Einar you helped us, and he'll give you treasure and silver, and you'll never have to see Thorir again."

"Shut up," he said.

He dragged her towards the biggest house, which was still half the size of Einar's great house. Thorir must be somewhere in there, probably surrounded by his men. If she wanted to do something to escape, it had to be now.

"I will curse you," she said. "You know I'm a witch, right? I'll curse you. I'll ask the Norn to weave into your destiny that your male bits turn green and dry out. You'll never be able to—"

A hard smack on the back of her skull made her teeth clank. Holly rubbed her head. So pretending to be a witch only worked with small boys. Where was the pregnancy test when she needed it?

They entered the house. It was dimly lit and, like all houses in the Orkneys, windowless. The room was full of men who were eating. The sour odor of unwashed bodies mixed with the heavy, sweet tang of mead.

On the other side of the room, Thorir sat on a large, wooden chair that resembled a throne. The chair was decorated with bones of all sizes, including the skulls of animals. As far as she could see, there were no human skulls, but a shiver ran through her, nevertheless. Thorir leaned on the arm of the chair, a horn of mead in his hand. As soon as she entered, his eyes were on her, and a small, lazy smile touched his lips.

Holly straightened. She wouldn't give the bastard the satisfaction of seeing her afraid.

Thorir stood up, nodded to the guard, and walked to the back of the house. Just like in Einar's house, there was a wooden wall and a door. If he wanted her to be alone with him...

A chill went through her as the door opened. She had been alone with him already. Einar had saved her. This time, if five days had truly passed, it was unlikely he'd find them or come in time.

But she had the needle.

Inside, there was a large bed, a hearth, several chests, and a small table with a chair. Holly's neck and shoulders hurt from forcing herself to keep her chin up. Her feet were as heavy as bricks, her lungs contracting for breath, her fists clenching.

The guard left the room, leaving Holly alone with Thorir. He was armed with a sword and an ax, and there were two axes and a shield hanging on the wall. What could her bone needle do against such weapons and a man twice her size? She could grab one of the axes, though, and...

And do whatever it took to save Svanhild and her baby.

The thought gave her strength. A she-wolf, she reminded herself. Einar said she was a she-wolf.

She needed to believe he was right.

"You bastard," she said. "What do you want with me?"

"I need you to tell me some things." He approached her and tried to take her by the arm, but she jerked it away.

He grasped her strongly this time, fingers digging into her flesh, and made her sit in the chair. Holly's hand crawled towards her thigh, where the needle was hidden on the other side of her apron.

"Why do I have the feeling you are not going to make this easy?" he said.

He grabbed her hand and didn't let go this time. He held it to the arm of the chair and wrapped a thin strap around her wrist, the leather digging into Holly's skin painfully.

"What the hell! Let me go!" Holly cried.

He repeated the process with the other wrist, and Holly kicked him in the shin. He fell back, surprised, a small trickle of blood crawling from the corner of his mouth. He smiled, amused, and as he was about to get up, Holly stood with the chair attached to her arms and swung it at him with her body. Thorir jumped back and yanked the chair by the leg, sending her tumbling to her side, one of her wrists falling at an awkward angle under the heavy chair. Blinding pain shot through her arm.

Thorir lifted the chair so that she was sitting again.

"I am enjoying your adorable act of defiance," he said. His smile was gone now, despite his words, but he was still relaxed. "But you are making it worse for yourself. I will have no mercy for you, witch. And you cannot win. You lost the moment I saw you. You belong to me. I will do whatever I please with you."

He took his short sword out and put it to her throat, the cold edge biting into her skin. His face hung close to hers, his mead-scented breath tickling her. His blue eyes pierced her.

The sword still at her throat, he brushed her hair back gently with his other hand, sending a cold shiver through Holly.

"I will get the answers now. And then I will send you to Odin as my gift." He cupped her face. "I am almost tempted not to and keep you for myself. Hmmm, you are a beautiful woman with such passion. Once you are disciplined, I can only imagine the nights I'd have with you."

He sank to his knees and began tying her ankles to the chair.

"If you move your leg, you'll get a wound so deep you'll bleed to death like a goat. We shall talk now, and later, maybe I shall allow myself one delicious bite before Odin has you whole."

"Go to hell," Holly spat.

"Hm. No. I'd rather go to Valhalla."

He finished tying her legs to the chair and straightened up.

"So," he said. "I saw much while I was hiding on Mainland. I saw the number of men Einar has and his weapons. I know what ships he has. I now have all his silver and his most precious possessions, including you and his daughter. What I still do not know is what arrangement does Einar have exactly with King Harald? Are Harald's reinforcements coming? The king's envoy, Solver, left. Is he coming back with more men?"

Holly clenched her teeth. "I'm not telling you anything."

He slapped her, hard. Her head shot to the right, her ears ringing, pain radiating through her skull.

"You will," he said.

She slowly turned to him. "Go. To. Hell."

Another slap, and this time, on the other cheek. He hit her so hard, her head spun with lancing pain. Oh God, her pain and distress couldn't be good for the baby, could it? But she just could not make herself shut up and take it. Besides, something told her if she was polite and silent and sulking, she'd make it worse. And she needed him off-balance. She needed to try to kill him if she wanted to protect her child and everyone she loved. If she simply escaped, Thorir would never stop chasing her as long as he lived.

"Why did the king's man leave? Is he bringing more men?" Thorir growled.

He was losing his nonchalant mood now and getting angrier.

"Yes, for God's sake!" she cried. "He's coming with a huge army, and he's—"

"Liar. You think telling me what I want to hear will make it easier?"

He grabbed the chair and tossed it across the room, together with Holly, as though it were just a heavy sack. She flew, her heart freezing in her throat, and hit the stone wall with her head and her side. The impact knocked the wind out her and deafened her. Her head detonated in white-hot pain. The chair broke apart, and something sharp pierced her side.

"She is useless." She heard Thorir mutter before opening the door. "Bring me the girl. Then the witch will talk."

# CHAPTER TWENTY

JUNE 9

OVER THE PAST FEW DAYS, Einar and his men had looked through every inch of land in the Orkneys, fighting the outlaws Thorir had abandoned in his escape. Yesterday, one of the men Einar had injured, spat out spitefully that Thorir had founded a new base on a farm in the Shetland Islands.

Einar was a fool. He should have gone to the Shetlands right away. The islands lay farther north from the Orkneys and Bretland, and therefore, were less likely to be controlled by anyone. Einar had not even touched them yet. He would not be surprised if the islands swarmed with outlaws and bands other than Thorir's.

Now the island with the farm lay ahead. Einar's ship, *Sea Bear*, which Thorir had stolen, was docked at the jetty.

"Faster!" Einar barked, and the men pressed on the oars. People on the island ran, preparing to fight Einar and his men.

"Let's get these pieces of shit," Einar cried. "Find my wife and daughter."

The ship thumped softly against the jetty. Arrows fell on them like rain, and men put their shields up. Some cried in pain as arrows hit their aims.

But they advanced.

They cut their way through Thorir's forces, losing men. The outlaws outnumbered them, but they were scraggly and poorly fed compared to Einar's men. Cries and thumps of iron against wood filled Einar's ears.

Einar caught one man and held him by the neck. "Where are they, my wife and daughter? Tell me, and I will give you a painless death."

The man pointed at the main house, and Einar slit his throat like he would a slaughter animal, giving the least suffering he could.

"To the main house!" Einar called. His men advanced.

The door opened widely. Inside, Thorir's men formed a shieldwall.

Behind it stood Thorir, with Holly and Svanhild.

Holly was bleeding from the head, half her face caked in blood. Einar's fists clenched, his blood raging for revenge. Svanhild was all right, just scared, her eyes wide. Thorir held a scramasax to the girl's throat.

Fear prickled Einar like a thousand needles.

"Only you, Einar," Thorir said, keeping his sword at Svanhild's throat. "You must come inside alone."

Einar spat on the ground and looked at his men.

"Keep your ears open. If you hear the slightest distress, if he kills me, come in. You must protect Svanhild and Holly."

He walked in and the door shut behind him.

❄

HOLLY'S HEART thumped as she studied Einar in the doorframe, his face and leather armor sprayed with blood, his hair wet, his eyes a promise of death to Thorir. He'd come for them. He'd fought for her and Svanhild. Her prayer to see him again, if only just for a moment, had come true. She hoped it was the enemies' blood and not his.

Their eyes locked, and in his, she saw pain and fear and hope and tenderness. Everything stood still. An invisible message passed between them. He was here for her—for them—and he wouldn't let anything happen to them. They had to play together as a team—she had to trust him.

And she did.

Her heart sang, expanded, beat harder and faster against her rib cage.

Unnoticed by anyone, her hand, now free of the chair and the leather strap, went under her apron. She carefully removed the long, thick needle. She kept it under her apron for now and gathered her strength to strike at the right moment.

"Give me back Svanhild and Holly," Einar said when the door closed behind him.

Thorir chuckled.

"Do you have the gold?"

"Yes. Back at the ship."

"Gunnar, go check," Thorir said.

One man left the formation.

"How did you find me?"

"One of your men betrayed you. But this was one place I should have checked first."

"You should have. I guess you are not as wise as some people think you are. Not as wise as a true Odin's descendant would be."

"I guess not," Einar said. "But at least, I do not smell like a troll's turd, and keep my home clean."

Thorir's face fell. "Enough jokes. Disarm him."

Holly watched with horror as one of Thorir's men approached Einar, who willingly gave up his sword and his shield.

"Will Solver bring back Harald's army?" Thorir said. "Your women refuse to tell me."

Einar's mouth pressed into a thin line. "Did you do that to Holly?"

"She did not want to be friendly."

"You will pay for this. Do you want Odin to notice you? I will make him notice. A bloody eagle will fly you to him."

The smug smile fell off Thorir's face, and he frowned. "You do not threaten me. I have your daughter and your wife here."

He pushed the blade a little harder into Svanhild's neck, and Holly's fist clenched around the needle. She wasn't standing close enough to do anything without attracting his attention.

Einar's face was a mask of fear and fury. He jerked forward, helpless, but was stopped by one of the men in the shieldwall with a hard shield hit to the chest.

Holly moved forward instinctively, her wounded side hurting.

The door opened and Gunnar returned. "There is no gold, Lord," he said.

Thorir's face distorted into a red mask of fury. "Where is that gold, Einar?" he yelled.

"Needle," Svanhild whispered, and her hand searched Holly's.

The blood drained from Holly's face. Svanhild? Was she ready to do this?

"Now," Svanhild whispered.

Holly passed her the needle, her hands shaking. Oh, you brave, brave little girl. You little Viking.

"The gold is hidden." Einar took a step forward, almost pressing into the shieldwall.

"You fucking liar!" Thorir yelled and pulled Svanhild closer to him, the edge of his sword pressing against her face now.

That was when it happened. In one swift movement, Svanhild turned towards him. She pulled back her arm and stabbed him in the forearm with the needle, sinking it deep into his flesh. He dropped the sword, clutching at his bleeding arm. The girl must have punctured an artery. He pressed his other hand against the wound, disoriented, shocked.

This was it. Now or never. Holly grabbed the short sword he had dropped and swung it, planting the edge in his neck. The man's face distorted in enraged surprise, blood flowing from the wound like a small waterfall. Then he fell, unmoving.

Thorir's men eyed their dead leader as though they were witnessing the end of the world.

"Lofarr!" Einar yelled and kicked the shield of one of Thorir's warriors. "Inside!"

The door flew open, and Einar's men spilled inside the room. The skirmish began, filling the space with yelling and the thumping of shields, swords, and axes.

The outlaws had lost the will to fight, though, and quickly gave up, asking for mercy.

Holly's hands shook as she stared at the dead body, still astonished at what she had done. She felt as if she were looking at herself from the side. She had just killed a man.

Well, he'd had it coming. She'd never let anyone hurt her baby, Svanhild, or Einar.

Einar pulled Svanhild and Holly into his arms, his dear, warm, familiar scent enveloping Holly, plunging her into the comfort of what felt like home.

"You are alive," he whispered, and kissed Svanhild on her

head, then Holly. “You are both alive. Let us go home. I will never let any harm come to you again.”

# CHAPTER TWENTY-ONE

JUNE 10

EINAR'S WARM, strong hands were around Holly, his hard body pressed against her back, his chest rising and falling in rhythm with her own as she lay in their bed. She inhaled the familiar scent of stone dust, ever-present in the house, and the scents of woodsmoke, leather, and iron, and the smell of cooking that always reached the bedroom, courtesy of the thin walls. The near darkness was soothing, with fires dancing on the walls, and the sounds of people cooking and eating together in the main hall, which made her feel at home.

Finally home.

No. She didn't want to think about it now. Even though the merger and her work were no longer the most important things to her, she still needed to leave for the sake of her baby.

Her head still felt like it were splitting in two, her stomach cramping, her side aching. She had felt like a puddle of goo the whole way back from the Shetland Islands. But now, being in Einar's arms, her strength was coming back to her.

"You stopped shaking," Einar said. "Are you feeling better?"

Even his voice was soothing. Like home. Like the bowl of delicious chicken broth with noodles that the cook had made, specially for her, and which stood steaming on the stool by the bed. Holly let out a long, gentle breath. People here were so kind. She had taught the cooks how to make simple noodles the day before she had been kidnapped, and they'd remembered her mentioning that she liked to eat chicken noodle soup whenever she felt like she needed comfort or was sick.

The moment they'd seen Einar carrying her in his arms, Bera had said, "Go slaughter a chicken," and Holly had known they were going to make the soup. Her eyes filled with tears. She brought Einar's arms closer.

"You make me feel better," she whispered. "Did Svanhild go to sleep all right?"

"Yes. She fell asleep the moment her head touched the pillow."

"Good job."

"It was all my fault, Holly. Had I been more careful—"

"You were careful. And it wasn't your fault. It was Thorir's. You couldn't have known—"

"No. I could have. But he paid for what he did to you and Svanhild."

Holly shivered at the thought of Thorir, how the heavy sword had sunk into his flesh. His surprised, pained look. The blood.

Still, she was safe now, and apparently, so was the baby. She'd do it all over again if she had to. Maybe she was a she-wolf.

"I should have searched better," Einar said. "I would have discovered the cave where he was hiding. And even if I hadn't, I shouldn't have left only a dozen men guarding the whole village. And even if not that, I should have thought of the Shetland Islands right away. I should have guessed they would pick the most remote islands with the fewest people. But I could not think. It was as though he had taken all of the breath out of my body, all of my ability to think straight. As though my soul had left me. Taking Svanhild and you—"

She buried herself deeper into his spooning body. If she could, she'd wrap him around her like a blanket. His words strummed a chord deep within her, and it sang, vibrating, reverberating, tickling her with joy.

Healing her.

Einar turned Holly towards him and cupped her jaw. His gray eyes burned with such gentleness that Holly's chest squeezed, and her head spun. Or maybe it was just the concussion.

"My heart is filled with you, Holly," he said. "The thought that you are stepping on the same ground as I, breathing the same air, it is like you are giving me a gift that I can never repay. Like you—" His voice broke off for a moment. Holly's heart pounded hard in her chest. He let out a small, shaky breath. "Like I lost the ability to breathe long ago, and you are helping me learn it again."

Tears filled Holly's eyes. No one had ever said things like that to her before. It sounded like he loved her...

Her stomach squeezed in excited anticipation.

But a voice inside her head that sounded like her mother, one she knew all too well, said, "Or is he just feeling guilty? Be careful. Men do not fall for you. Men do not choose you."

She tensed and closed her eyes, a tear crawling down her cheek. Today, she'd choose to ignore that voice. Today, she'd choose hope.

"Einar, I—" She opened her eyes and wanted to tell him he

was the best thing that had ever happened to her when a sharp contraction made her double up and yelp in pain. She felt a gush of something warm between her legs.

"Holly?" Einar sat up, his voice thick with worry.

Holly lifted the blanket and her skirts.

The insides of her thighs were smeared with fresh red blood.

"No, no, no!" Holly cried, the tears spilling down her cheeks, her chest tearing apart.

Another sharp wave of pain cut her lower belly in two.

"Aaaahhh!" she moaned. "Bera! Fetch Bera, Einar! Something is wrong! Something is wrong!"

"The babe is still inside of her, but she might be losing it," Bera told Einar. "If you ask me, she probably will. That amount of bleeding...her injuries..."

She shook her head, mournful creases forming around her mouth. Bera and Einar stood outside his bedchamber. Inside, Holly was finally resting. The sharp pains had reduced to the level that she did not scream anymore.

"I gave her a calming tea with valerian," Bera said. "What Thorir did... It was too much for her."

Einar wiped his forehead of sweat. His whole body was as tense as a ship's ropes in a storm.

It was just like eight years ago. Waiting outside of the chamber where, on the other side of the door, the woman he loved was being tortured, bleeding, and possibly losing her life and the baby's. When it was clear she would not make it, he had been allowed in. The squall of pain covered him as he remembered blood in the bed and on Agdis's thighs, the unbearable screams of pain against which there was no cure, the air in the room, humid and thick with the scent of iron and sweat.

Bera had drawn runes on Agdis's wrists and belly with charcoal.

The same runes were now on Holly, too. ᛈ, *perthro*, the rune of luck on her belly. ᛒ, *berkana*, the rune of fertility on her right wrist. Finally, ᚹ, *wunjo*, the rune of joy, laughter, and happiness on her left wrist.

"I called upon all three goddesses, Freyja, Frigg, and Eir," Bera said. "It is in their hands now."

"Will she die?" Einar asked.

Bera sighed, her stern face softening, and grasped his hand.

"It is unlikely," she said. "I will clean her womb if she loses the babe. It is very small. It will pass on its own, or I will take it out."

Einar nodded. The walls, the ceiling, the ground were closing in on him. He could not breathe—sharp pains were mincing the cavity of his chest like the blade of a new scramasax.

"I will go and make another tea for her," Bera said.

When she left, Einar touched the door handle and saw that his hand was shaking. He clenched his fist and took a deep breath, chasing the images of a dead Holly away.

He entered, and she looked at him. She was pale, her eyes wide.

"I was hoping you would be asleep," he said.

He stood at the edge of the bed, unable to move, to go any closer. Afraid to hurt her with a single touch.

Afraid that, somehow, he would do something to make it worse. That she would begin screaming from pain again.

"I can't," she said. "I'm so terrified I'll lose the baby."

He swallowed, chasing away the burning in his eyes. The

terrible, unspeakable, cowardly thought that scratched at the back of his throat.

"Maybe it would be for the best," he said.

She sat up, her face as white as cotton grass. "What?"

He lifted his chin, his lips tensing, twisting. He heard his own cruelty, and he hated himself for it. But fear, the desperation of meeting that one enemy he could not protect her from —childbirth—left him helpless.

"Maybe it is for the better if it ends now," he said, "rather than waiting, hoping, and then losing you and the babe when there is nothing I can do to help you."

She exhaled a shaky breath, her hands clutching the blanket at her stomach.

"You don't mean that, Einar. You don't really wish this baby to die. Do you?"

His body was burning. Turning to ashes. Being plucked by ravens.

"I do not wish death to *you*," he said. "I need *you*. That babe —if it kills you—"

His voice broke. No words came, held back by a rock that formed in his throat. Holly's cheeks were flushed, tears filled her eyes and streamed down her face. Her mouth opened in a grimace of pain, her chest rising and falling.

If it killed her, he would be nothing. He would be better dead, too.

"Do you realize," she said, "that everything that I do is faulty. That there's been an error, some sort of mistake, in every relationship I've ever had? I couldn't conceive at first. Now I can't hold on to the baby. Will I ever do anything right?"

Her chin trembled, and her voice shook.

Einar wanted to go. He was making it worse. "I am hurting you," he croaked. "You need to rest."

But she cried.

"I can't even perform this one thing all women are supposed to do. The one thing that doesn't depend on your education, on your income or your brains. The most physical thing in the world—procreation. And I'm failing even there."

She put her head on her knees, hugged herself, and wept. Einar could not leave her like this. He sat on the bed next to her, wrapped his arms around her, and pulled her close to his chest. He thought she would push him away, but she clung to him as if he could save her from drowning.

"You have no faults, Holly," he whispered. "I would take you whole. I would take you with every single thing you think is wrong with you. And I would not change a thing."

All he needed now was for her to get better. She needed a rock, and he would be her rock. He would be her anything, as long as she would live.

Even if that would mean putting her on a ship and taking her to back to her own time.

# CHAPTER TWENTY-TWO

June 15

"I think the babe is still there," Bera said.

She withdrew her fingers after doing a pelvic exam, and Holly covered herself, the corners of her mouth crawling into a smile for the first time in what felt like forever.

"Really?"

After five excruciating days of fear, of flinching from every cramp and expecting to wake up to a pool of blood, the news was like lifting a dark, heavy blanket.

"Yes," Bera said. "There was no more bleeding. Your womb is closed. It feels like you are keeping this babe, for now."

Holly inhaled sharply and looked at Einar. He had been so supportive of her for the last few days, hadn't left her for a moment. She wanted to hug him, to kiss him, to feel his strong arms around her. She had thought that since he'd been so supportive, maybe he realized he wanted this baby after all...

Her smile fell.

He looked as though Holly was torturing him. His face was grim, his mouth curved in a tight, mournful line.

Right. All that she had thought was an illusion. She was pregnant, and he didn't want her to be.

Holly's chest hurt, as though scalded by boiling water.

When Holly and Einar were alone, she sat straight up in bed, thinking carefully about what to say. "You were taking such good care of me for the last five days. I thought you might have changed your mind about..."

He tensed, became like a giant statue.

"You needed all the support you could get," he said.

Now that the most precious thing in the world was likely to be okay, the man she had fallen in love with was withdrawing.

The door flew open and Svanhild rushed in. She jumped into the bed with Holly and hugged her. "Am I to have a brother or a sister?"

Her eyes shone. Her father's eyes were so different—a stormy sky. Holly straightened her back and pressed down a tight knot in her throat, her eyes burning from tears she was desperately holding back.

"It looks like it, Svanhild. But we need to wait and see. It's still very early."

Svanhild hugged Holly's waist and pressed an ear to her stomach. "Hello there," the girl whispered. "You do not go anywhere. I will pray to Freyja and Frigg for you."

Holly brushed Svanhild's hair with one hand. A single tear she could not stop ran down her cheek, and she quickly wiped it.

"Father, do you want a son?" Svanhild asked.

Einar jerked back as she said that, his body rigid, hidden agony making his eyes dark.

"Svanhild, do not stick your nose in the adult business," he said, voice lashing like a whip.

Svanhild's eyes widened, and she stopped breathing for a moment. Then she slowly crawled back from the bed.

"Forgive me, Father," she said and left the room.

Holly's heart bled. "Why do you have to be so harsh with her? She didn't do anything. It's not her fault you're so—"

"So what?"

"So cruel."

She saw his jaw tighten, his fists clenched.

"It is better to be cruel now than get her hopes up for nine months only to be crushed. I do not want her to end up like me."

Holly shifted in the bed and stood up next to him. "Like you?" she said.

"I want her to be happy."

"Are you not happy?"

"I was," he said, glancing at her gently, his eyes caressing her. "But I will not be in two days."

Holly frowned. "Why?"

"Because in two days, the ship will be ready, and it will take you to Scotland, or wherever you need to go."

Holly wanted to shrink into a ball and cover herself from all sides.

"Because I'm pregnant?" she whispered.

"Because you do not belong in my life," he said. "I should have never given in. I should have never looked at you. I should have never kissed you. Everything between us was a mistake. A joke of the gods. You have always said you needed to go back home. That was the agreement from the beginning."

Every word lashed her, hitting right where it hurt the most. Just like Jack and every boyfriend before him.

They all thought she wasn't good enough. They all thought something was wrong with her.

And now, Einar did not want her. The one who hurt her the most. The one who mattered the most. The one she loved.

The father of her future child.

Einar knew he was hurting her. Like she had not had enough pain in the last few days. Being kidnapped, abused, then almost losing the babe...

And now this.

But better now than later. Now, while the babe was still small. Now, when he knew Holly and the babe had the best chance under the care of healers in the future. Now, when he knew he loved her and that letting her go would be safer for her.

"Fine," she said. "I can't believe I actually considered staying with you for a second, abandoning my career, my life, my parents..."

She'd considered staying? The words hit him in the gut.

The images of them together—a healthy babe, maybe even the three sons she had mentioned; a prosperous jarldom here on the Orkneys; Svanhild marrying a good man that Einar approved of; long, hot nights full of fire; talking to Holly or just being by her side—brought him a feeling of peace.

But these were only dreams. The hard truth was, she would likely be dead—she and the babe—and he would be destroyed. And he still needed to be here for Svanhild.

"You should not have considered it. I also should not have asked you. Had I known that you would get with child, I would never have stayed in one room with you. Gods know, it is impossible to keep my hands off you."

"I'm such an idiot. Such an idiot. You know what, Einar, you are terrified of losing people. I understand. But your daughter is growing up without the love and support that she needs. She has no mother, and the way you're behaving, she might as well not have a father."

Anger rumbled through him. How dare she? But deep down, part of him knew she was right. She had hit right where it hurt the most.

"She has a father," he croaked. "Everything I do is for her safety."

"You cannot keep her safe from everything. A life spent avoiding things that hurt us—it's a life not worth living. Yes, your wife and your baby died. But you loved them. And now you're trying to live the rest of your life playing it safe? That is not the Viking I know. Not the Einar I fell in love with."

His throat went dry. "In love?"

"Yes, Einar, rejoice. I fell in love with you. I'm happy to carry your child. You won. Like all men, you see things that are wrong with me, and you used me. You couldn't keep your hands off me, but you can't imagine risking pain for me. Yes, if I stay here, I might die. But I'd rather die after being happy, after carrying a life in my body, after spending the happiest nine months of my life with you and Svanhild, than crawl back into my safe shell in Orlando."

Einar's throat hurt. He watched as she got back into bed and cuddled into the blanket. He wished to cover her with his body instead.

"I'll be ready in two days," she said. "I can go tomorrow as far as I'm concerned. Don't let me stop you preparing the ship."

"Holly—" he said. The hurt in her voice, her withdrawal, her words... They set his soul in turmoil.

"No," she said. "You don't want to be with me. And I don't want to be with a man who is selfish and cowardly enough to refuse the life he really wants—with a wife and future children. You're a warrior, you face death almost every day. How is this different?"

# CHAPTER TWENTY-THREE

June 17

The whole village had gathered at the jetty to wish Holly well before her journey, their faces sad. Holly stood on the pier, waves splashing against the longship behind her. She hadn't seen Einar since last night. Now she searched the crowd and the landscape for his tall figure. She needed to do the most difficult thing—say goodbye to him. A movement among the villagers caught her eyes, and the crowd parted. To her astonishment, Einar came to her in full armor and his bear cloak.

He stopped before her, making her stomach squeeze at the sight of the stern, gorgeous face that had become so dear. "I will take you there. I must make sure you are safe," he said. "You and the babe."

Holly's nausea returned at that. Or maybe it was sorrow. Sorrow because by demonstrating that he cared, he showed her what she had lost. What they both had lost. How could he show he cared yet force her to go at the same time?

"We'll be fine," she said. The idea of spending another day or maybe longer with him—seeing him but not being able to touch him, to kiss him, to talk to him like they used to—was torture. "Stay here. Don't feel obligated—"

"I am going and that is final," he said, moving past her to the ship.

Her chest shrank and hurt. She turned her attention to Svanhild. The girl's eyes were bloodshot and watery, but her back was straight, her chin high. She walked to Holly.

"Please do not go, Holly," she said.

Holly crouched before the girl to be on her eye level. Holly's eyes blurred, and she fought the tears. She brushed a hand gently over Svanhild's golden hair.

"I must, Svanhild," she said. "If I could, I would stay. But that's impossible. I'm so sorry that I'm leaving you. I love you very much, sweetheart." She kissed Svanhild on the forehead. "Take care of your father, okay? He seems grumpy, but deep down, there's no one more important to him than you. He is doing everything for you. The whole reason he's taking care of the Orkneys is for you. Remember that."

Svanhild hugged her, hot tears wetting Holly's cheek. "Please come back. Or take me with you to the future."

Holly's chest hurt as though blown to pieces by a grenade. Her face burned, tears streaming down her cheeks. "I can't, honey. Your place is here and mine is there. Leaving you is one of the hardest things I've ever done. I'll think of you every day for the rest of my life. I'll tell your brother or sister about you. I'll pray you find a good husband or have a great adventure if that's what you want to do."

She leaned back and took Svanhild's face in her hands, looking into her hazel eyes. "Whatever you do, stay strong. Stay true to yourself. And don't let anyone tell you that you're not good enough. Because you are. You're amazing. You saved my life, your father's life, and the life of my baby."

Svanhild nodded, her expression serious, tears still falling.

"I think my mother sent you to me," she said.

Holly smiled, a rush of gratitude expanding her lungs. "No, sweetie, it is you who were sent into my life to make it better."

Holly kissed the girl on the cheek and hugged her for the last time. "Stay well, Svanhild."

Then she stood up and walked to the ship. It was as if invisible rubber bands were pulling her back to the village, as if a knife were cutting those strings, sending explosions of pain through her with each one it severed. She was leaving a part of her soul on this island. With Svanhild. With Einar. With the villagers.

She boarded the ship, wiping her tears away, ignoring Einar's pained look, and went to sit in the bow. Soon, they departed. Holly gazed at Mainland, Orkney, etching every green curve and every gray cliff into her memory. She only looked away once the land was no more than a thin line on the horizon.

The whole day, Einar was on one side of the ship and she on the other; although, she swore she could feel his heavy eyes on her. When night fell, he came and sat down next to her.

"You will freeze," he said. "Let me warm you."

He was right. She was freezing. She shouldn't even talk to him. But she craved his touch like a plant craved water and sun. For the baby, she told herself. But deep down, she knew it was because this would probably be the last night she'd ever spend with him.

"Okay," she said. "Only because I am freezing."

He lay back against the curve of the ship and opened his arms to her. She went into his embrace, inhaling the dear scent of his skin—the masculine tang of sea, wood, and leather. He covered them both with his bear cloak, his heavy arms around her, his hard body under her cheek, and she immediately relaxed and stopped shaking.

One last moment of joy, she told herself. *Pretend that we are okay. Let this night stretch an eternity. Listen to his strong, fast heartbeat. Engrave it into your memory to remember it during the lonely nights to come in Orlando.*

She felt his face move to the top of her head, and she thought he inhaled the scent of her hair. Maybe he still wanted her. Maybe he enjoyed their time together. But it didn't matter. They had no future for so many reasons.

But they had now. They had this night.

In the darkness, under the stars, the sea air fresh and tickling her nose, he was close. He was home. She cupped his jaw and he closed his eyes. His brows drew together, an expression of agony creasing his face.

"What are you doing, Holly?" he asked.

"I don't know," she said. "I just...I can't believe I will never see you again. That it's the last time you're holding me. That—"

A low growl, almost animal-like, escaped his throat. He opened his eyes, and they were full of heat. "Last time," he said. "I will have you for the last time. The gods owe me that. Yes?"

She shuddered from a thrill of excitement at the idea of having his strong arms around her again, of him being inside her. She was crazy, probably, to make love to a man who didn't want her in his life. But she was hurting, and the only balm that would ease her pain was him.

Instead of answering, she kissed him, and he responded by devouring her as though he had been hungry for a hundred days and she was a feast. His arms crushed her to him, so hard she thought he might crack her ribs. Heat rushed through her where their bodies melded, where their lips touched, and their tongues played a desperate, needy game with each other.

Einar turned her away from him and lay on his side behind her, cupping her breasts. The touch spurred her desire even more, and she bit her lip to stop herself from crying out. He ran his hands down her waist and laid them gently on her still flat lower belly, over the place where their child grew inside of her. Holly held her breath.

Then Einar pulled her even closer, lowered his head, and began kissing the side of her neck. He brushed the length of her leg until he reached her ankle, then pulled the dress up to her hips. His hand was hot, his skin a little calloused.

Oh God, she was going to miss these touches. She pressed her behind into him and felt him, long, hard, and ready for her.

"Is no one going to hear us?" she asked. The rest of the crew were sleeping a little farther away, scattered along the length of the ship.

"If you do not scream," he rasped, his voice charged with promise.

He gently cupped her sex, making her entrance hot and wet. Then he moved his fingers to her folds and spread them. Holly gasped, absorbing the intense pleasure. One of Einar's fingers found the clit, which he knew well by now, and began lightly rubbing it. Holly arched her back and hid her face in the fur cloak, suppressing a moan.

"That is right, my sweet," he whispered. "Try to keep quiet."

"Ahhhh," she moaned softly as pleasure built within her.

His other hand went between her legs from behind, and one finger dipped into her sex. She cried out a little louder now, her insides clenching around his finger. But it wasn't enough.

"You," she said. "I want you. I need you. Fill me."

He withdrew his hands, and she felt him rummage with his trousers. Then his hard, heavy erection was against her, and she wiggled to let him where she wanted him—deep within. He directed his erection, and with one sleek movement, slid into her. She gave out a satisfied moan as he stretched her, filling her hungry, sensitive flesh.

He didn't move for a moment, and Holly pressed against him. It was as though an invisible cocoon covered them, as though they weren't two separate people anymore but one. As though he didn't fill just her body but her heart and soul.

Then he began moving, pounding into her softly at first, then harder, spilling ecstasy like she'd never felt before. He put one hand on her shoulder, the other on her hip. He thrust into her again and again, building pressure within her, soaking her in sweet agony. She muffled her moans in the fur, but she felt like they were rocking the ship so hard, everyone must know what they were doing.

And then the buildup was there—right there. She stood with him at the edge of a cliff, looking into the shiny blackness of the sea below, and the moon and stars glittering above, and with one final thrust, she fell.

She convulsed, unable to stop her outcries this time, but letting the bear fur swallow them. He was grunting, too, his whole body hard and stiff, groaning softly in her ear. He came in her this time. Oh, how good it felt, how satisfying, how much she missed the pleasure of having him come inside her.

When they were both panting softly, he tucked her against his chest without pulling out, and Holly didn't remember the last time she'd felt so peaceful, so good, and so loved. Without realizing, she fell asleep.

Holly woke up warm and a little sore in her neck. Einar's eyes were on her, and she wanted to smile at him because she loved waking up to see his face. But his eyes were sad and so full of anguish that she immediately remembered everything. They were on the ship, and she was going back to her own time.

She cleared her throat to say something to speak, to beg him to let her stay.

"Land," he said and sat up, gently pulling the cloak from her. "We have arrived."

# CHAPTER TWENTY-FOUR

Near the Village of Tongue, Sutherland, Northern Scotland

Standing on the grass-covered slope, Einar's stomach tensed as though someone had stabbed him in the gut with a scramasax.

Here it was, the place where he would lose the woman he loved forever, green-brown hills rolling above unforgiving rocks till the eye met the horizon.

"I think it's over there," Holly said, the wind playing with her short locks, making her hair flutter around her beautiful face.

She pointed at the hill where Einar thought he saw a charred building.

She resumed walking up the slope, and Einar stopped himself from saying, "Do not go. Do not leave me." The night with her had shown him everything he was going to lose forever. The overwhelming feeling of peace, as though he had finally arrived home.

Seeing her walk away was like losing a dear part of himself.

But the decision had been made. And if he wanted her to live, her place was in the future, where healers would make sure she lived through the birth of his child.

She had said three sons.

Maybe this was one of them.

His feet felt as if they had put roots into the ground, but he forced himself to walk after Holly.

He took in every movement of her legs under her dress, every swing of her arms as she walked, hoping to catch the slightest sign of hesitation...a sign that she would turn back and tell him she would not go anywhere no matter what he had said.

But she did not hesitate.

Finally, she reached the top of the hill, and Einar stopped some distance behind her. The sea was dark and vast beyond the cliff, and she stood bewildered on the grass and rocks, looking around. She had said something about a tree—but there was no tree that Einar could see. What did it mean? He dared not hope.

The village on the left looked empty for the most part; although, Einar thought he noticed some movement flickering behind the corner of a house before it disappeared. This must be the village that Thorir had raided when he had taken Holly hostage.

"There's no tree," she said.

Einar opened his mouth to tell her they could continue searching; although, a part of him hoped they'd never find it.

But from the corner of his eye, he saw someone standing ten paces away from Holly, an old woman.

She wore a regular Viking apron dress, her white hair done in a braided crown around her head. Colorful necklaces of beads hung suspended between her brooches. Her face was wrinkled, but her eyes were not those of an old woman—they were far too full of life and burned with curiosity.

He put his hand on the handle of his ax. Norn or not, goddess or elf, he did not know what her intentions were, and he would protect Holly from any being—human or supernatural.

"Hello, Holly," the woman said. "Hello, Einar."

"Hello," Holly said, then added to Einar, "Meet the Norn, Ms. Verdandi."

Verdandi was the Norn responsible for what could be. Einar's skin prickled and crawled, and his jaw fell open. Was he, indeed, in the presence of the most powerful being in all worlds, the being who not only defined his destiny, and destiny of all men, but of the gods, as well? Of all nine worlds?

He still did not remove his hand from the ax. He did not trust the woman. Maybe she was just an imposter. Holly's safety was his priority.

"Are you certain?" he asked.

"Yes. She was the one who sent me here."

Einar closed his mouth and swallowed. The Norn smiled serenely and walked towards them. Something golden glistened in her hands.

"You came here to go home, Holly?" the Norn said when she stopped before them.

"Yes," Holly said. "But, there's no tree."

"No, there isn't," the Norn said. "But I am here. I want you to know that if you decide to go now, it will be very hard to return here."

Holly nodded. "That is for the best. There is no future for me here."

The Norn looked pointedly at Holly's stomach. "I doubt that, dear."

Holly glanced at Einar, who could not stop staring at the

Norn. Although he knew, logically, it was better that Holly went, he hated that the Norn was about to take the woman he loved away from him. She might as well be a dragon who was about to breathe fire.

"No. It is best that I go. Einar doesn't want me here, and I should get back to my life. My family and friends are probably worried sick."

"It is better for you," Einar said, his chest tightening with pain. "It is better for the babe. You have good healers there. That is what matters."

The Norn exhaled with a chuckle. "Jarl Einar of Orkney. Destiny has given you the perfect woman, and yet, you are pushing her away. And you, Holly, are so afraid no man will ever want you that you are leaving the man who does."

He might be pushing Holly away, but only for her own good—and for his. He was choosing life for her and not death. He was protecting her and himself. He wouldn't survive if she died in his arms.

"You're wrong," Holly said, her eyes filling with tears. "Going back is the best thing for everyone."

Einar's body tensed and ached from the pain in her voice. She needed to go. He both wanted and hated the idea.

Holly held her hand out for the spindle. "Give it to me, please."

No. Not yet. "Holly—" Einar said, his voice thick, his chest tearing apart with worry and pain.

"As you wish, dear," the Norn said. "As they say, you are the master of your destiny."

She placed the golden spindle into Holly's hands.

Einar jerked forward one step, instinct calling for him to push away her hand and let the spindle fall.

Too late.

She was disappearing, dissolving like a cloud in the wind.

No!

Holly looked back at Einar. Agony gnawed at his heart. He reached for her—to hold her, to keep her—but his hands went through the thin air, right where her arm used to be.

"Holly!" he cried.

He was still looking into her eyes, the last part of her that he could hold on to as she disappeared.

# CHAPTER TWENTY-FIVE

Orlando, Florida, June 19, 2019

"Oh, Holly, you came!" cried her assistant, Kenny.

He jumped up from the desk, his handsome face a combination of relief and worry.

Holly marched right to the glass door of her office, through which she could see Alan Murphy, her COO, sitting at her desk, talking on the phone. He was a bit over forty, overconfident, and could sell a horseshoe to a horse. He was good at his job, but his ambitions went higher.

Holly was dressed in her war gear: a bloodred blouse, burgundy tailor-made suit, and the highest heels she owned. Einar's armor was leather and iron. This was hers.

And she'd come to take back what belonged to her.

Yesterday, she'd flown from Edinburgh to Orlando. The whole way from Tongue was a blur. She hurt inside so much she hadn't known where she was going. She'd been surprised to find the car she had rented—the key had miraculously appeared in her hand the moment she'd emerged. Maybe the Norn had mercy for the pregnant, beaten-up woman and had decided to cut her some slack.

When Holly had stepped inside her apartment, she'd felt like she was in a dream. Like everything she saw around her was a hallucination. The full-wall windows, the spotless white-and-chrome furniture, and the crystal chandeliers, which seemed too bright after the stone, grass, and earth she had seen for weeks on the Orkneys. She'd lowered the shades and gone to take a shower. Then she'd taken another pregnancy test, which had been positive. She'd called her ob-gyn and wanted an appointment today, but the earliest they could accommodate her was in two weeks.

Then, once she'd had a big steamy cup of fruit tea and ordered tacos from her favorite Mexican place, she'd finally gathered the strength to call her mother.

"Holly?" her mother had answered, voice strangely quiet and weak. "Is that you?"

"Hi, Mom," Holly said, already tensing, ready for a berating.

"Are you all right?"

"Yes, Mom. I'm fine. How are you and Dad?"

"Paul!" she cried. "It's Holly!"

Dad picked up the second phone. "Holly? Are you all right?" he said, his voice fast and loud.

"Hi, Dad. Yes, I'm fine. I just got back."

"Where the hell have you been?" Mom yelled. "We were worried sick! I was about to fly to Scotland to look for you! Not a word for more than a month! How could you?"

"Gemma..." Dad said. "Holly, she's right. We were worried. Where have you been?"

"Sorry, Dad, I got a little carried away with my Scottish adventure. I didn't mean to worry you or upset you. I'm fine. I guess the stress and the pressure made me act out of character, and I just...I just disappeared. I'm sorry, Mom."

"No, you did this on purpose!" Mom cried. "You wanted to hurt me. You wanted to run away..."

Holly sighed, her eyes blurring with tears. She didn't have the capacity to deal with this. But she needed to calm down the people who loved her.

"No, Mom, I'd never hurt you intentionally. I couldn't get you a message, okay. If I could, I would have. Please, I'm very sorry. I'm also very tired. I just wanted to let you know I'm back and I'm well. I can't talk about it now. Let's meet tomorrow, and I'll tell you what I can. Please."

"Let me come over now," Mom said. "I'll make you lasagna. We'll talk."

"Let's do it tomorrow, Mom. I'll come visit you for dinner, okay?"

"What about Sunnybeach Developments?" Dad said. "Did your deal happen?"

"I'm about to find out."

"Okay, Holly," he said. "We love you. Get some rest. And call the police to tell them you're fine. They searched for you."

"But, Paul—" Holly heard her mom's protest before the line was cut off.

Holly put the phone aside and sat without moving for a moment. She understood how her mom felt. How it must have completely crushed her, not knowing if her daughter was dead or alive, if she was being treated badly, or if she was in trouble. She hated not knowing how Svanhild was doing. She hated thinking that something might happen to her unborn baby. But if she told the truth to her parents? No one would ever believe her. Her mom would probably have her committed.

She gulped the tea and exhaled.

Then she'd called Kenny to find out what was going on in the company.

And now, here she was—angry, ready for battle, and torn by a never-ending pain in her chest.

Alan glanced up as she swung the glass door open, his face first showing an expression of shock, then defensiveness, then a polite smile.

He stood up, barked, "I'll call you back," into the phone, and his fake smile broadened. "Hey, Holly! You're back. Good to see you. Where have you been? What happened to you?"

Holly came into the room and stopped right in front of him. She put her briefcase on the glass table with a bang.

"I've been having a little trouble in Scotland. I couldn't get out, but now I'm back."

He nodded. "I'm happy to let you know that in your absence, I took over. Although because you disappeared, the deal has not yet happened. But I'm working on closing it."

"Right," Holly said, crossing her arms over her chest. "I hear that's not the only thing you're working on."

He relaxed his tie a little. "What do you mean, Holly?"

"You're trying to get my job."

His eyes hardened. "Look, you were gone. Not a word. We thought you were never coming back. Someone had to do something."

Holly clenched her teeth. Anger roared in her. She'd stood up to Thorir—twice—and come back alive. She was ready to eat Alan for breakfast. "Of course," she said. "And you were only too happy to take the opportunity and put yourself forward for my job with the board of directors."

"No one knew if you were coming back. The company needs to continue running."

Holly sighed. He was right. Someone did need to continue

managing the company. Wouldn't she have done the same in his place? Why was she so angry with him?

Because she needed an outlet, someone or something to concentrate on, rather than thinking of Einar, Svanhild, and the Orkney Islands. Rather than letting the black-as-night heartbreak suck her in. She needed to distract herself from wondering if she'd done the right thing by leaving.

She had.

Einar didn't want her. This is where she belonged. She'd ensure the best future for the baby and continue doing what she was great at—running a business.

"Well, I'm here now," she said and took a deep breath. "I can take over. Why don't you fill me in?"

"Does the board know?" he asked.

"No one knows yet. I wanted to see the situation for myself first. Kenny is letting them know as we speak." She nodded to Kenny, who was on the phone.

"They might not be thrilled you're back..." he said.

"Why do you think that is? Because you almost ruined a perfectly setup merger?"

He paled a little. "I have everything under control. I was just on the phone—"

Holly lifted her chin. She loved this—problems being thrown at her, the thrill of finding creative solutions running through her veins like electricity. "Why do they want to pull out of the merger?"

"They didn't say it with so many words. But they've been stalling signing."

"Are they talking to someone else?"

"I don't know."

Holly resisted rolling her eyes. Of course he didn't. He'd probably scared Kamasaki Enterprises with his upfront manner. Kamasaki was a smaller construction company that specialized in commercial real estate and had been started by a Japanese immigrant twenty years ago. The company still had a softer, more subtle business culture with a lot of context that one needed to understand. Alan, with his straightforwardness and stubbornness, was probably not even able to notice the differences.

"I'll talk to Mr. Kamasaki," Holly said.

The day passed quickly.

Well. Not quite.

It passed in fits and starts. Holly had to talk with Mr. Kamasaki, meet the lawyers, talk to the board, meet the employees, and look through documents. But the moment she had a free minute to herself, to even allow herself one thought, the same one rolled over her like a wave of pain, dragging her into another world.

Einar.

She missed him so much, as though without Einar, she lacked an element vital for her survival.

His dark-blond mane of windblown hair came to mind, his stormy gray eyes. His stern face softening when their eyes met. His hands...

Oh God, his hands...

His big, warm, skilled hands commanding her body like it belonged to him. His mouth kissing her, tasting her, devouring her. And then him entering her, bringing her to previously unknown peaks of pleasure.

His respect, his appreciation of her household management, how much he loved her cooking.

How much he hated that she was pregnant...

She forced herself to stop thinking about Einar and to come back to the present moment. She looked desperately for something else to concentrate on—anything to chase him from her mind. From her heart.

And she dove into work like never before.

July 3

She almost missed her ob-gyn appointment, and rushed out of the office at five o'clock. Her stomach quivered in nervous waves as she sat in the waiting room. A few other women waited alone, but many had their partners with them, and Holly couldn't help feeling jealous.

How would it feel to have Einar with her, looking forward to this baby as much as she was? To share those expressions of love and happiness with each other, as though they couldn't believe this miracle had happened to them?

For Einar, it was a curse, not a miracle.

God, what the hell was wrong with her that she had fallen in love with a man who didn't want to be with her because he got her pregnant? And was she some sort of masochist that she missed him and wanted to be with him anyway?

"Holly," the nurse said, and Holly jumped up. Her heart beat in her ears as she went to find out if she'd lost the baby or if it was alive.

When Dr. Felder was doing the ultrasound, Holly held her breath, waiting to hear the verdict. "I was so surprised when you called with the news," Dr. Felder said. "But congratulations. There's the pregnancy," she said when, on the monitor, a big black balloon appeared in the middle of gray matter. She moved the wand some more. "And, there is the baby."

To the right side, against the blackness, floated a little gray jelly bean. Holly exhaled a breath she didn't even know she'd been holding.

"And there's a heartbeat!" Dr. Felder said.

Holly chuckled, tears springing from her eyes.

"There is?" she whispered.

"Yes. It's a viable pregnancy. How did you manage after seven failed inseminations— Never mind, it's none of my business."

Holly swallowed. Maybe there was nothing wrong with her in the end. All she'd needed was a man born hundreds of years before her. The man she loved.

"I suppose I just got lucky," Holly said.

"By the size, it looks like you're six weeks along. Is that right?"

"Yes, sounds about right."

"We'll confirm the due date closer to twelve weeks, but for now, it looks like you're due on February twelfth."

Holly wiped away a tear. In February, she'd meet this baby.

"Again, congratulations. I'm just so thrilled for you. I know how much you wanted this."

Holly smiled, but her expression was strained. She'd need to learn to live without Einar. To think about what she would tell the baby about its father. To figure out what to tell her parents and her coworkers.

And to accept the reality that this would be her life.

Always missing something.

Always missing someone.

Because even though she'd finally have the family she wanted, it wouldn't feel complete without Einar and Svanhild.

# CHAPTER TWENTY-SIX

THE ORKNEY ISLANDS, July 31, 880 AD

EINAR GAZED at the endless blue sea and threw the long grass he was chewing away. He had been looking at the sea every day since he'd come back from Sutherland.

Every day since the woman he loved had disappeared right in front of him.

And taken his heart with her.

What was he looking for in the sea? For a boat that would bring her to him? For an outlaw ship that he could chase? That would provide a distraction from his excruciating thoughts about Holly. Fishing, hunting, and weeding simply did not cut it.

The long grass whispered behind him, and he turned to see Svanhild. She came and sat down next to him, facing the sea. Einar watched her for a moment. Sometimes he couldn't believe this wondrous little creature was his daughter. She was so pure, so pretty, so gentle and kind. The gods had given him the best daughter he could wish for.

Only he had never been the best father.

"Did you want to talk to me, Father?" Svanhild asked.

"Yes," Einar said. "Now that the islands are free of outlaws, we can finally start thinking of the future. I am jarl now. The lands are ours. We can start inviting more people to farm and settle here. We can start establishing neighborly relationships with Sutherland and the other kingdoms. Do you know what that will mean?"

Svanhild glanced at him, wide-eyed. "What?"

Einar felt his face warm. Holly would have been very handy to explain the delicate matters he needed to talk to his daughter about. He did not know what he was doing.

"You are a child still, but in five or six winters, you will be of an age to marry."

Svanhild's eyes were huge now. "What are you saying, Father?"

"I want you to be prepared and to start thinking about what kind of husband you want. When we visit neighbors, keep your eyes open."

"But I don't want a husband."

Einar glanced at her, a little embarrassed. Maybe he had started this talk too early. She was frowning.

"Not now, of course. I am speaking of the future. You are my only daughter, and I want you to marry well and be happy."

"I meant ever. I do not want to marry at all."

Einar turned to face her fully now, the feeling that he had done something very, very wrong swelling in the pit of his stomach. "You do not know what you speak of, child. Why such harsh words?"

"I do not want to die giving birth, Father, and leave my

child like my mother left me. And then Holly left me because you chased her away, afraid that she would die, too."

Her words pounded at Einar's head like a blacksmith's hammer against an anvil. This was what he had done wrong. He had given her a bad example. An example he did not wish her to repeat.

"Svanhild, I have made mistakes. Do not take on my misgivings as your own."

"Would you wish me to die giving birth?"

"What? Of course not."

"Then, there you go. I do not want to be treated by my husband like you treated Holly. I do not want him to make me leave when I get pregnant."

Einar clenched his jaw. "If anyone makes you leave or abandons you or harms you in any way, they will answer to me."

"And what if I come to you with child, would you make me leave like you made Holly leave?"

His mind raced, imagining a pregnant grown-up Svanhild coming to him in tears. The image tore him apart.

"I will never make you leave. There is nothing that you could do that would make me reject you, Svanhild."

She eyed him. When had she become so grown up? Had separating from Holly made her so sad? So wise?

"But you rejected her. And my brother or sister." She sounded so hurt, her voice full of resentment.

Einar almost winced from the blame in her voice. But part of him was strangely glad Svanhild was telling him what she thought instead of keeping silent and shying away from him. He guessed he had also become more open with her. He had been talking to Svanhild more often and telling her good-night stories every few days. He had never been as close to Svanhild as he had become this past moon. And it was all thanks to Holly, he knew.

"They are safer in the future," he said, his voice a quiet rasp. "The healers are powerful there. They will not let anything happen to her."

Svanhild turned to him, her eyes bloodshot and full of tears. "But what if they would not have died here? Many women give birth, and they and the babes live. My mother gave birth to me. Are you not willing to see the chance of that?"

Einar sighed and turned away. He was willing. He dreamed about Holly, alive, blooming, the babe in her arms. Dreamed about another child running around, giggling with Svanhild as he started a fire to roast a fresh herring. He had longed for a big family for a long time. He wanted to leave the Orkneys not just to Svanhild, but to more children. There was enough land for everyone. The feeling of peace and well-being that had begun to settle over the village once the outlaws were gone had not touched him.

There could be no peace and no well-being without Holly.

"There is a chance of that, yes, Svanhild. And I sincerely wished that it would have been so."

The truth was, Holly had wanted to go from the beginning. But he had almost convinced her to change her mind. If she had not gotten pregnant, he would have done everything in his power to get her to stay. He would have showered her with gifts and made love to her with such passion that she would see the gods. He would have told her how he really felt. That he loved her. That he wanted to dedicate his whole life to worshipping her, body and soul.

And now his life was incomplete. And it would never be complete without her.

Svanhild sighed and looked towards the sea.

"If she was still here, would you change your mind?" she asked. "Would you let her stay? Would you risk it?"

Einar clenched and unclenched his fists, helpless.

How was it possible that his ten-winter-old daughter showed him exactly what he was so afraid to see for himself. Something that Holly had warned him against, too, before she left—that he was wasting his life by hiding from pain, by running away from happiness.

Without her, every day was like dragging himself through a snowstorm. Every day was lifeless, soundless, tasteless. And every night, he lay in his bed, unable to sleep, just like he had for all those years after Agdis's death. His hand would brush against the cold sheet where Holly used to lie, searching for her, but knowing all too well, he wouldn't find her there.

Even the villagers missed her. The cook made her favorite chicken broth sometimes, with those noodles Holly liked so much. The whole house enjoyed it and called it "the Holly soup." Although no one asked him about her, he knew the household servants talked about her when they were alone. He could hear them through the wall of his bedchamber.

They missed her, too.

And her advice to use peat instead of wood would get them through the winter and warm them for years to come. The Orkney and Shetland Islands were all rich in peat. They only needed to dig it and dry it, then store enough for winter.

They would not have anything to worry about.

And he knew he was not the most cheerful person. But ever since Holly had left, the feeling that he had lost something vital would not let him go. Like part of a ship had been destroyed. And no one knew how to fix it, but the ship was sinking. Fast.

And it looked like Svanhild, the little boat, was sinking as well.

Einar sighed and closed his eyes briefly. He'd had everything and he'd lost it. But did he regret marrying Agdis? Having Svanhild? Marrying Holly?

The answer came simple and clean.

No. Never.

He had been happy for that time. He had been complete. His life had been worth living.

He would do it all over again.

Why? Because despite the heartbreak, despite the desperation, despite the grief, the days when he had been happy with Agdis shone brighter and tasted richer than the sad days. Because he had Svanhild as a result.

And because he had received the greatest gifts of all—he'd met and gotten to spend time with Holly. Gotten to call her his. Gotten her to answer him with the same affection he had for her.

"I would change my mind, Svanhild," he said. "I would beg her to stay. And I would pray to the gods every day to protect her and the child."

"Truthfully?" Svanhild said.

"The risk of heartbreak. The risk of death. It is all worth it, Svanhild. The days, the months, the years that you get with the person you love, with your children. Why else are we here?"

Svanhild visibly swallowed and shifted closer to him, then leaned against his arm.

"I was a fool," Einar said. "If I could search for her and ask her to come back, I would. I would accept the risk of her dying in childbirth if she was willing to accept it. If there was even the smallest chance she was somewhere in this time, I would have fallen on my knees and begged her to stay with us already."

Svanhild eyed him, her mouth open.

"Do you truly mean that, Father?"

"Yes." He dared to wrap his arm around his daughter, so small and delicate, and kissed her on top of her head. She leaned into his embrace, making the area around his heart warm and melt.

"And I hope that you will not make my mistakes," he said. "Choose love, Svanhild. No matter how long or short. Choose love."

# CHAPTER TWENTY-SEVEN

ORLANDO, Florida, August 31, 2019

"MORE SALAD, HONEY?" Holly's mom asked.

Holly looked at her across the table, her dark-brown eyes, her curly gray hair, her slender figure. Mom had always been petite and healthy, and Holly had been raised health conscious. But now she was in her fourth month of pregnancy, and all she wanted was pizza, a huge juicy steak wrapped in a roasted chicken, and at least a bucket of mashed potatoes with gravy.

But Mom had read that if Holly ate a low-GI diet, it would give the baby a healthy weight, lower Holly's blood sugar, and not let the baby get used to carbs. So the dinner consisted of a dressing-free spinach salad with avocado, braised salmon—which made Holly nauseated like all fish—and steamed green beans. After dinner, Holly was stopping at a fast-food restaurant.

"Yes, thank you, Mom." Holly held out her plate, which still had half her salmon on it. At least the salad didn't make her want to vomit.

Mom flashed a businesslike smile. "Eat, eat. You're eating for two."

"Yes," Holly said. She could eat a double portion now, but no way was she touching that salmon again.

"So, honey, how is the merger going?" Dad said.

Holly smiled at him, grateful to change the topic from food, which always set Mom lecturing as though she was a trained dietitian.

"We signed last week. Kamasaki Enterprises is now our subdivision for developing malls, shopping centers, retailers, and such."

"You saved the day again, didn't you?" Dad said.

"I'm sure it was a team effort, like with everything. Right, hon?" Mom said.

Holly was reminded suddenly of those family dinners during her high school years when Mom had asked her how her day had gone, and she had told her it hadn't gone great—high school had been a difficult time. Then Mom had started to look for reasons it hadn't gone great, and the main reasons were always in Holly. Something she'd done, said, or thought had led to worsening marks, conflicts with her classmates, people making fun of her. Holly even remembered being in the same situation Svanhild had been in, with the bullies in the village.

Was it at this comfortable, cozy, family table that Holly's belief that she was never good enough had been born?

And who said that she wasn't good enough? That anything at all was wrong with her? She was pregnant. She'd met the love of her life—who she felt loved her, too. She'd withstood a psycho Viking who wanted to murder her. She'd saved the merger.

What part of any of that was wrong?

"Not really, Mom," Holly said. "The team effort without me, lead to Kamasaki almost pulling out of the deal completely. Only when I came back and intervened, were we able to complete it after all."

"Oh. Right, honey. Just don't be arrogant, okay, sweetheart?"

Holly clenched the fork and put it down. "Mom, I'm not being arrogant. I deserved this. It was thanks to me because I built a rapport with Mr. Kamasaki. Because I understand their reasons for merging, which weren't written anywhere on paper. And because I could deliver the promises in the merger. Alan Murphy and the team were not able to complete the deal without me. It's not arrogance. It's a fact."

Mom listened to her with wide eyes, then bowed her head slightly and returned to her food. "There's no need to raise your voice, Holly. I didn't know."

"No, you didn't know. But you assumed. Like you always assume that things go wrong because of me. That something is always wrong with me."

Mom swallowed and blinked. "What?"

"Men leave me because I'm too strong, according to you. I couldn't get pregnant because I didn't eat well and drank too much coffee. And on and on. You always find something to point at. You make me feel like I'm defective. Like there's something fundamentally wrong with me, in everything I do. Even my real parents didn't want me..."

Holly knew she had gone too far. Mom gasped and jumped up from her chair. Dad froze and paled, looking at Holly helplessly and with such pain that she felt as though her words were cutting him in half. Maybe it was the pregnancy hormones, but tears burned Holly's eyes, filled them, and began streaming down her cheeks.

"I'm sorry," Holly said, covering her eyes with her hands and leaning on the table.

Mom pulled a chair up to Holly's side and hugged her, the small but strong hands pressing her tightly.

"They were idiots if they didn't want you," Mom said. "But we wanted you so much, it hurt. Who wouldn't want you, baby? You're beautiful, and the smartest person I know, and the strongest. You don't give up, and you work as hard as ten men. And, of course, it was thanks to you, that merger. Anyone with a brain could see that. And I'm sorry I'm so hard on you. I just want you to be careful, to consider all the consequences. To not get ahead of yourself. I never meant for you to feel defective. Just careful. All mothers want their children to be safe. That's all I want for you, honey."

Holly bawled in her arms, and Mom, who always smelled like vanilla, felt like a safe haven. Holly felt Dad moving and taking the chair on the other side of Holly, then his big, warm hand lay on her back.

"But why did he send me away then?" Holly whispered. "If nothing is wrong with me, why do men not want to be with me? Not men, one man. Him. Why did he send me away, that buffoon?"

"Who?" Mom said carefully. "The father of your child?"

Holly nodded and straightened, wiping her eyes. She'd never told her parents what had really happened. She'd just mentioned that she'd met someone in Scotland and accidentally gotten pregnant. Then she'd asked them not to interrogate her any further until she was ready to talk. After Mom had carefully asked if Holly had been raped, and Holly had assured her that she had been perfectly safe, Mom had let the topic go. Although, Holly sometimes felt Mom was having a hard time swallowing her questions. But a hard glance from Dad usually did the trick.

"Yes. I fell in love with him, and I think he loves me, too. But he sent me away, although I really wanted to be with him. He has a daughter, and she's so sweet."

"Who is he?" Mom asked. "What does he do?"

Holly sighed, wiping her eyes. Should she just tell them? "He's a Viking jarl. I traveled back in time to the ninth century, and he saved me. He's my husband."

Mom raised her eyebrows. "I'm sure it's some sort of a metaphor, that time travel. Do you mean he has a castle? Lands? Is he a nobleman?"

Holly shrugged. If she insisted on her explanation, they'd think she was having a nervous breakdown. "Sort of."

"And you married him?" Dad said.

"Yes. We never divorced. He just... He sent me away. I mean, I wanted to come back. I'd probably have come back anyway. I needed to close the deal. But the main reason I wanted to leave was that I was terrified to fall in love with him even more and for him to end up rejecting me and leaving me like every single man in my life before him."

"Why did he send you away then?" Dad asked, and for the first time in her life, Holly heard a note of steel in his voice.

"He—his previous wife died in childbirth together with his second child. He was terrified that would happen to me, too. He never wanted to get another woman pregnant. He had thought I'd leave eventually and wasn't interested in a real marriage with him, so he'd believed I wouldn't want children."

"But he loves you?" Mom said. "He's just afraid to lose you. You and the baby?"

Holly pursed her lips. "I think so, Mom. I think he loves me. Which doesn't guarantee he'd never leave me like other men. Jack loved me in the beginning. So did Ryan."

"Honey, we love you, and we'd never want to leave you or let you go. The right man won't, either. Jack, Ryan, all those others were idiots. I'd have killed them if I had known what kind of nonsense they'd put in your head. Maybe you should call this man. Invite him and his daughter to Orlando. Have him meet us. He's your husband... And why is it that you didn't invite us to the wedding?"

"It was very rushed. He needed to be married to fulfill a certain contract."

"Okay. Well, you can maybe do a second ceremony for us here. But call him first. Surely, he's regretting it. Besides, you're not going to die in childbirth. No one dies in labor these days."

Yeah. These days.

Holly wished she could call him.

Her parents had accepted half the truth so well. Could she tell them the whole truth? Since today was all about opening up and letting go, she'd tell them.

"I can't call him. Believe it or not, I did travel back in time. He lives in the past."

Mom and Dad were both quiet.

"Sweetheart, I don't get it," Mom said. "You sound crazy, but I know you aren't."

"Yeah. I'm not. I'll just tell you what happened and hope you believe me. There's nothing I can do to prove it to you. So either you trust me or you don't."

And then she told them. About Ms. Verdandi, who turned out to be the Norn, about the tree and spindle, and about Thorir and Einar and Svanhild and the village. She told them about her wedding and Thorir's raid. About his kidnapping her and Svanhild, and how Einar saved them. And about her returning to her own time.

When she finished, her parents' eyes were as big as saucers, and they were looking at each other. Everyone was quiet. Holly gave them time to process the news.

Dad shook his head. "You should write a book, Holly. It would be a good one." He stood up. "I'll clean the dishes."

But Mom stayed. She covered Holly's hand with hers and looked deep into her eyes. "Is this true?" she asked.

Holly nodded. "Yes."

Mom nodded back. "As insane as it sounds, I believe you."

Holly's chest lightened as though a heavy weight had been lifted. "Really? Why?"

"Because I know you better than anyone else," Mom said. "And you love him, don't you?"

"Yes."

"I love your dad. It killed me not to be able to give him a child. If you love Einar and he loves you, you should go back to him, honey. Your life will be a misery without him. You'll regret it. And there's nothing worse than a life of regret. I don't want you to live that way. All I wish is for you to live a full and happy life."

Holly's eyes filled with tears again. "Mom, you have no idea what that means to me."

Mom squeezed her hand. "I never thought you were defective, dear. You're the most perfect person I know. I'm so proud to be your mother. And since all I want is your happiness, this is my warning—you'll regret it if you don't try to find the man you love."

Holly sucked in a breath. "But my job..."

"Does it make you happy? Do you feel satisfied and fulfilled?"

Holly thought about it. What her job had been for the past couple of months was a drug. A drug to help her forget Einar. But the feelings of loneliness and emptiness were everywhere, and they were only growing. She loved managing and organizing. She loved structuring things to make a profit.

But she loved Einar more.

And she could do all that back in the Orkneys. She could help Einar grow trade, manage his household, and improve things in the Orkneys. She could help him make his lands the most prosperous they'd ever be.

And she could give him his son. If she was the woman destined to give him three sons, the first one was growing inside of her right now.

But what about him abandoning her? Her being faulty and not good enough?

No. She was good enough. She had always been good enough, she realized now. If he did abandon her, it wouldn't be because she was defective. And she would always have herself. Her own approval was the only thing she had ever been lacking, and the only thing she needed.

"No, Mom, I don't. And you're right, I do need to try. I'll only live a half-life if I don't. I'm going to find my husband."

# CHAPTER TWENTY-EIGHT

THE ORKNEY ISLANDS, September 21, 880 AD

EINAR GENTLY PRESSED Svanhild's shoulders down. She held a bow in her left hand and pulled back the string with the right, aiming her arrow at the straw-filled target Einar had made using a broken shield covered with linen.

In the middle, he had drawn a large circle with a piece of coal. The target was between two tall, flat stones that stood like columns. Farther away were the third stone and the fourth stone, which was thick and had a round hole pierced through it. Einar had a mind to call it Odin's stone and give praise and do blots for Odin's sake there. After all, the god had helped him rid the islands of outlaws and get Svanhild and Holly safely away from Thorir.

"Soften your shoulders, Svanhild," he said. "Pretend that you are reaching for something, but only with your arm."

Svanhild's shoulders sank down as her arms straightened.

"Good," he said, pride filling his chest. Svanhild was a smart and capable girl. "Now, do you see your target?"

She nodded slightly.

"Good. Let go when you are ready."

She exhaled and relaxed her fingers. The string made a swooshing sound and the arrow flew. A moment later, it pierced the middle of the target.

Svanhild's lips spread in a broad smile, and her chest puffed out slightly. She could be very proud of herself. She had asked Einar, after their talk on the cliff, if he would teach her to protect herself. She had wanted to ask him ever since he'd rescued her and Holly from Thorir but had only been brave enough recently.

At first, Einar's instinct was to say no—he hated the idea of his little girl with a weapon in her hand. But if he thought about it without losing his head from worry about her, he knew he wouldn't be able to protect her every day. The world was full of men without honor, and a Viking always had an enemy, even if he might not know about them. And his daughter had shown tremendous courage by protecting Holly and herself using a simple binding needle, making him proud.

He had agreed. He would start with archery and then teach her melee combat for self-protection. If his daughter wanted to learn a warrior's craft, he would grant her wish. Even though it pained him to think that she had to do this at all. He wished to keep her completely safe.

Which he knew was impossible.

"I hit it!" she exclaimed, then turned and hugged him.

Einar had not expected the gesture, and she'd kicked the air out of his lungs, not from the physical impact but from emotion. She had not touched him since she was but a babe, and warmth spread through him, pouring over his heart like a healing balm. He wrapped his arms around her and pulled her close, not quite believing she was, indeed, hugging him.

"Thank you for teaching me this, Father," she whispered. "I did not think you would agree."

"You were victorious over Thorir Treebeard without knowing any combat," he said. "You are brave. The least I could do is to teach you to protect yourself properly."

Einar decided to be brave, too, and kissed the top of her head. His heart was filled with love and gentleness towards his daughter, but his happiness had a bitter edge. The ache for Holly filled his whole body in a sharp wave of emptiness. If only she could be here. If only she could share this with him and Svanhild.

But he'd lost her and the babe, and he was the only one to blame.

He wished he could see her one last time. He would do everything to convince her to stay.

The autumn sun was warm today, and Einar prayed that it would stay warm for the harvest festival tomorrow. Solver would come tomorrow, and Einar clenched his jaw tighter, imagining what the skald would say once he found out that Holly was gone.

Then, behind the slight hill, he noticed two figures approaching—a man and a woman by the looks of it. Einar let Svanhild go and squinted against the sun, trying to see who that was. Loki must be playing with his mind because he thought the woman had bright-red hair.

Holly's hair. But this woman's hair was longer, almost reaching her shoulders.

He let Svanhild go and walked towards the two. The need to see if it was his imagination or reality pulled at his chest.

The woman seemed to walk faster, and he started running towards her, no longer able to stop himself. His heart pounded so hard he thought his rib cage would crack. His muscles prickled with pins and needles. He was a fool for even hoping she would come back. He was about to be disappointed like never before in his life.

But the green grass flashed under his feet, the blue sky brightened, and the sun burned him.

And then he was close enough to see.

Holly.

She was still a distance away when he stopped as though hitting an invisible wall, and he fell to his knees.

He watched her continue towards him, the beautiful smiling face and big green eyes, her shoulder-length hair moving in the wind. Her cheeks were flushed, her lips red. Something was different about her—maybe it was the feminine roundness of her figure. Her belly swelled under the green apron dress, telling him she still carried his child, and his eyes burned with tears of joy that he pressed back.

He could not stop looking at her. He could not take his eyes away even for a moment, afraid that she was, after all, a vision.

But the flash of white linen and golden hair that swooshed past assured him that she was not. Svanhild did not fall on her knees...she ran full-on towards the woman.

"Holly!" Svanhild bellowed. "Holly! You came back!"

Then Einar saw Svanhild almost knock her to the ground as she pinned herself to Holly, wrapping her arms around her waist. Holly beamed even brighter, still looking at Einar, but hugging and kissing Svanhild back.

"I'm here, sweetheart," Holly said, her voice shaking and tears falling down her cheeks.

Next to Holly, Solver stood with a satisfied smile. He raised one hand in greeting to Einar, and somehow, seeing Solver made this real. Holly was here, by some miracle, and by the goodwill of the gods.

Einar pushed himself up and forced himself to walk towards her, feeling as though logs were attached to his feet.

"Sweetheart, give me a moment to talk to your dad," Holly said, and Svanhild let her go, still beaming. She stood next to Solver who was watching them. Holly locked her eyes with Einar's and walked towards him.

They came together in the middle. Einar failed to find words, his throat tight. Instead, he devoured her with his eyes and knew without a shadow of a doubt that he had never seen anything more beautiful.

"You came back," he croaked.

"Yes," she said.

Then nothing. She swallowed. Maybe she struggled to speak as well.

"Why?" he asked.

"To be with you," she said. "To be your wife. To be Svanhild's mother. And the mother of this one." She rubbed her swelling belly. "If you'll have me, of course. Will you?"

Einar's world shifted. It brightened and gained colors. His whole body flooded with relief, with love like the warmth of golden sunlight, the lightness of good mead, and the freshness of a morning wind.

Would he?

Finally, the emptiness in his chest began filling, the sensation of completeness like a smooth patch over the tears and scars in his heart.

"Will I have you?" he said and pulled her into his arms.

She felt so right, so small and gentle and warm pressed against him. How he missed the feel of her against his body, the sound of her voice in his ears, the delicacy of her lips.

He kissed her, sinking into her taste. Her lips were like flower buds, soft and full. He kissed her gently, but hunger was already stirring within him—hunger for her body, hunger to connect with her soul to soul, hunger that had not stopped since the moment he first saw her.

He withdrew, and she gazed at him, breathless.

"Is that a yes?" she asked.

"I love you more than life itself," he said. "I love you so much that I will have you in any way I can."

She smiled.

"It is a yes," he said.

She nuzzled against his chest. "Thank God. I was worried you'd send me away. But I would have stayed until you changed your mind. Because I love you, too, Einar. I'm ready to be with you, even if at some point you get tired of me or learn something about me that turns you off, and you leave me."

Einar chuckled. "Woman, you speak nonsense. I will never get tired of you, and nothing I learn about you will make me leave you. As long as the gods allow me to love you and have you by my side, I will."

Her eyes filled with tears. "Even though I will need to give birth here?"

He swallowed, a stone of fear forming in his chest as he imagined her in the pains of labor.

"I will have you as long as the gods allow. I will do a sacrifice each day if necessary. But if your time comes, I will cherish every day spent with you. Every word you said. Every kiss and touch you gave me. And I will love you until the last moment of my life."

She bloomed. "And I will, too," she whispered. "And I will, too."

Svanhild appeared next to them and hugged them both, her face bright and happy. "Solver told me how you got here."

The skald took a step closer to them.

"Holly appeared a week ago in Avaldsnes," he said. "She was on a trade ship from Sutherland, wishing to ask King

Harald to give her a ship to come here. I was coming to your harvest festival, and so, I was fortunate to bring your beloved wife to you."

"Why did you go to Avaldsnes?" Einar asked. "Why not here?"

"No one was going here from Durness, but there was a trade ship bound to Avaldsnes, so I thought I'd ask King Harald. I told him you had allowed me to visit my family but that the ship that brought me was later destroyed in a storm, so I couldn't go back."

"How did you cross time again?" Einar asked.

"I had to track down the Norn. It wasn't easy. She was still in Scotland with another 'client.' She came with me to the same place we met her and gave me the golden spindle. I can't go back, though, she said. This was the last time. And I'm okay with it, Einar. There's nothing I want more than to be with my family. Here."

Einar felt a huge smile spreading his lips under his beard.

"So you can never leave?" he said.

"That's right."

He hugged his pregnant wife and his daughter. "Thank Odin."

# CHAPTER TWENTY-NINE

The Orkney Islands, February 19, 881 AD

"Not long now, dear," Bera said, barely throwing a glance at Holly from her knitting—no, not knitting, *nålbinding*. Bera looked so comfortable by the turf-burning firepit, which filled the bedchamber with a pleasant warmth. Einar was fishing in one of the lochs nearby, although he had been reluctant to leave her. Svanhild had asked him to teach her, and Holly had encouraged him to go.

Holly answered by moaning like a cow. She leaned against the bed, kneeling on the floor with soft furs under her knees, which was the most comfortable position to breathe through the contractions.

Not contractions, she corrected herself. *Surges*. That was what the book on HypnoBirthing said. Do not think of them as of pain, contractions, or anything unpleasant. They were strong energy surges, the intense waves she needed to ride by breathing deeply.

"Mmmmmoooooooo," Holly moaned on a slow exhale as intense pain shot through her round stomach.

She smiled, then laughed even through the surge, and the pain diminished.

"I do sound like a cow, don't I?" she said when the contraction had passed.

"Yes." Bera smiled. "You can sound like Hel herself if you like. Anything to make it easier for you."

"Did those books I brought give you any useful hints?"

Holly had brought several books on midwifery and even a medical book where there was a detailed description with pictures of a C-section. She'd verbally translated those books for Bera.

"That C-section part was interesting, but I will need to practice on the sheep and cows before I attempt anything like that on a woman. I do think it is a wonder what healers from your time can do. But we just need to rely on the gods and the Norns to weave us a good destiny."

Holly nodded. She must be crazy to be attempting to do this here. But she had made a decision, and she would stick with her man. She would breathe and relax and soften and trust her body to do the job. And very soon, she would hold her baby.

The next wave came, even more intense and longer than the previous one.

"Mmmmmmmmmmmmmmmmmmmmmmmmmmm."

Then heavy steps thundered from behind the wall, and the door flew open. Einar stood there, snow on his boots, his eyes big.

"Holly, are you—"

"Mmmmmmmmmmmmmmmmmmmm," Holly moaned. His fear was getting to her, making her tense, and her contraction felt more painful.

"She is," Bera said. "And you better get out."

Behind him, Svanhild stood, watching Holly with her eyes full of fear, too.

Holly exhaled and straightened up as the surge passed.

"Einar, Svanhild, everything is okay," she said. "If you want to stay, you can, but you must leave your fear behind that door. Here, there's no place for anxiety. Here, all I need is calmness, smiles, and laughter. Because I sound like a cow, and I'm not sure if you're ready to see your wife as a cow."

Einar swallowed and relaxed his face, then nodded.

"So, what's it going to be?" Holly asked. "In or out?"

"I will wait outside and make you your favorite chicken noodle soup," Svanhild said and disappeared into the room behind.

"What about you?" Holly asked Einar.

At first, Einar's gorgeous face was a grimace of anguish. Then something flickered through him, and his expression became decisive. "In," Einar said and removed his winter jacket.

"First, wash your hands," Bera said.

EINAR DID NOT KNOW how much time had passed since he'd entered his nightmare. Just like Agdis, Holly was suffering, torn apart by pain, and he could do nothing to help her. He could bring her water, hold her hand, and wipe her forehead. He could breathe with her and do those cow noises that made him think of blot sacrifices and of death.

And that made the ugly, cold fear in the pit of his stomach grow bigger and bigger.

Her *surges,* as she called them, were getting closer and closer together and longer. And she moaned louder.

"You're still terrified," she said after a particularly intense one. "I feel it, and it makes me tense even more. And if I'm tense, the labor will be longer and more dangerous. All I need is complete relaxation, an all-will-be-well mentality in the room. Got it?"

Einar nodded, not believing inside at all. How could he believe that all would be well?

"Make me laugh. Kiss me. Tell me a story. Just don't sit like an old dry stump and glare at me."

Make her laugh? How in Loki's name was he supposed to make her laugh when all he could think was, *please, Odin and Freyja, do not take her away from me.*

"I can kiss you," he said. "I can do that."

Holly smiled, and his world brightened. Agdis had never smiled during either labor. "Okay," Holly said. "Attaboy."

She was still kneeling on the floor, leaning against the bed. He sat on the bed and leaned towards her. He drew her to himself and kissed her gently, slowly, letting her know with his lips and his tongue how much he loved her.

"Mmmmmm." She gave a different kind of moan. A moan that he knew very well. A moan that stirred fire in his veins.

Bera coughed, and Holly and Einar froze, then giggled.

"Ahhhhhhhhhhhhhhhh!" Holly closed her eyes and breathed, but surprisingly, throughout the surge, she was smiling slightly.

Then, moments later, she opened her eyes and her smile grew. "See," she said, "that's way better."

Einar chuckled. "If kissing will save your life, I will never stop kissing you."

Holly laughed. Then her eyes dulled and she closed them, moaning again, breathing deeply. Einar watched, breathing with her, holding her hand. He admitted, inside, he was much calmer now. If he considered it carefully, this labor was different from Agdis's. But that did not mean it would end well.

He chased the thought away. He needed to believe it will be all right. The Norn had predetermined their destiny already anyway. He could only help Holly by staying positive. And by kissing her.

After what felt like an eternity, she opened her eyes. "I think it's time," she said.

"Do you feel you need to push?" Bera asked.

"Yes," Holly said.

"I will check."

Bera stood up, then knelt behind Holly and went under the skirt of her shift.

"Oh yes, girl," Bera said. "I feel the head. Push, dear, with the next surge."

Bera sat on the other side of the bed and held Holly's hand. "Lean on us," she said. "And just let your body do what it wants to do."

This had been when Agdis could not get the babe out. Much time had passed—days—and she had only writhed in pain until she'd died in his arms.

"Okay." Holly smiled. Her face was flushed, her eyelids half closed. She looked as though she were watching him from another world. "Here we go," she whispered on an exhale. Then she stopped breathing, squeezed Einar's hand, and tensed.

Her face reddening, she doubled up a little and grunted. Then she exhaled and sucked in air.

"Oh, man, this is a hard job," she said. "Can I have some water?"

Einar gave her the water, and she drank thirstily. She did not look like Agdis, who had been crying and in pain even between the pushes. Holly was calm and relaxed, just tired.

Einar had not been present for Svanhild's birth, but he imagined this must be how a normal labor went. He looked at Bera. Her eyes softened, and she gave him a slight nod.

"This is good," she said. "This is good."

Einar exhaled just in time to have his hand squeezed till it hurt. Then Holly began her long grunt again, her face tensing and reddening. A deep breath in, and again, the push.

Then she let go for a short time, her eyes still closed. "Einar, rub my back," she managed.

Einar was glad to be able to do something for her, anything to bring her relief. He knelt on the floor and began to massage her back, just the way she liked it.

"No, lower back, and harder," she said.

"Yes, Holly."

He did as she asked, rubbing her lower back in circular motions, and her head fell back. "Ohhhh, that's good," she said.

And so they went on, Holly, relaxing and softening, then tensing, shaking, reddening, and groaning. Einar did not know how much time passed. Bera checked under her skirt from time to time and did not say anything, but her face remained calm, and Einar did not inquire, not wanting to alert Holly in case something was amiss.

Her grunts were longer now, and soon, she was making soft, thin sounds every time she breathed out. Then, during one push, she cried in pain, and her head fell back. "Oh, make it stop! Make it stop!"

Bera pushed Einar away and sank under Holly's skirts.

"The head is crowning," she said. "You are going through the ring of fire, maiden. Go on. Just one or two more pushes and you will hold your babe."

Einar inhaled a shaky breath. Was this true? Was it almost

over? Would he not lose her? Bera held her hands between Holly's legs.

"Ahhhhhhhhhhhhhhhhhhhhh," Holly cried, making Einar's blood stand still.

"Give me clean linens," Bera said. "Quick."

Einar rushed to the small, neat heap of fresh linen Holly had woven herself. On top, laid a white thread and a red one. The white one would be used to tie the cord. The red one had an amber bead on it and would be tied around the babe's wrist for protection. There was also a black one, and Einar knew that Bera must have burned it earlier today in a ritual to drive away death and bad luck. Holly had woven the threads earlier during the pregnancy, under Bera's careful instruction.

Einar held the heap to Bera, and she took one linen and covered her hands with it.

"One more, girl!" Bera said.

"Ahhhhhhhhhhhhhhhhhhhh!" Holly cried, the sound a painful plea.

Then Einar heard a barely audible *pop* sound. He looked, and a small head was between Holly's legs. He felt as if his heart stopped.

"Good," Bera said. "You birthed the head. One more push and the babe will be in your arms."

Holly panted, her head hanging between her shoulders.

Then she gathered strength and grunted again, piercing the air with an animallike growl.

The babe slid peacefully into the clean linen in Bera's arms.

"That is it," Bera said. "Here is your son."

Einar watched as she turned the babe and slapped it gently on its little arse, and the boy cried. Einar's heart beat so strongly he thought it would jump out of his throat. The feeling of bliss and love spread through his chest, through his stomach, through his whole being.

"Help her to the bed," Bera said. "We still wait for the afterbirth, but she needs her rest now."

On weak legs, Einar helped Holly climb into bed. The furs were covered with a few layers of fresh white linen. The babe was still crying, attached to the cord. Holly looked into Einar's eyes and smiled.

And then he knew that he hadn't lost her. He kissed her, happy and delirious from the feeling of trust that filled his chest. He sat by Holly's side as she leaned back against the pillows, undid the straps of her shift in front, and cradled their son against her bare chest. Bera tied the white thread around the dark rope that connected Holly and the babe.

The boy was small and wrinkled and very pink. Holly covered him with a linen cloth and a blanket Svanhild had made. He stopped crying and nuzzled against Holly.

"He is looking for your breast," Bera said.

"Oh, sure, little boy," Holly said.

While she helped the babe find a breast and begin sucking, Einar could not stop admiring every little part of the image before him. His beautiful wife, his son.

His son.

Someone knocked and the door opened a bit. Svanhild peered inside, her eyes wide, full of both fear and curiosity.

"May I, Bera?" she asked.

"Of course, you may," Holly said. "Come meet your brother."

Svanhild jogged towards the bed and stood by Einar's side, regarding the babe with big eyes, then the happiest smile Einar had ever seen.

"He looks like you, Father. What will you call him?"

"We must wait until we bless him with water in front of the gods," Einar said. "But I already have an idea."

"What is it?" Holly asked.

She beamed at him, looking like a goddess of fertility, beauty, and femininity. Something had shifted in her—the small wrinkles around her eyes had softened, a glowing spark appearing in their mossy depths. As though she had learned the secret meaning of life and happiness. And she showered Einar in it when she met his eyes.

"Baldr," he said. "It means strong and bold, and it is also the name of the brave and handsome god."

"I love it," Svanhild said.

"So do I," Holly said, and her eyes filled with tears. "Thank you for giving him to me," she said to Einar.

"Thank you, wife," he said. "That is one son. Two more to go, according to your prophecy."

She grinned and leaned over to kiss him. "Happily, husband. Let's grow the tree of our family tall and strong."

Happiness flooded Einar's heart and soul as he met the soft lips of his wife. And he did not know if he tasted love, peace, or wholeness.

But he would take it all, for eternity, as long as he was with Holly and their family.

# EPILOGUE

Near the Village of Tongue, Sutherland, Northern Scotland, May 5, 882 AD

"This is it," Holly said to Einar, Svanhild, and Baldr. "This is where I appeared two years ago."

The wind blew in Holly's face as she studied the bare hill. By her side stood her husband, her daughter, and her son, all of whom she loved more than life itself.

Svanhild held a gray ball of fur with two giant, golden eyes —Loki, the cat. Though he seemed to be more like a dog, not wishing to separate from the girl for a moment.

Holly was pregnant once again, probably still in her first trimester—although, without ultrasounds and doctors, it was hard to say exactly because her periods had remained irregular.

The hill was still bare and treeless, and Holly felt she had made the right decision. The tree needed to be planted, or the future Holly wouldn't have a way to go back in time. Fortunately, Tongue bore no signs of the raid that had happened two years earlier and swarmed with the regular activity of spring as the villagers prepared to plant their crops.

Holly and her family were there to do a planting of their own. In one hand, Einar held a seedling of an ash tree and in another, a shovel.

Svanhild walked a few steps ahead. "Where was the tree? Here?"

Holly narrowed her eyes, trying to remember. "Maybe a couple of steps to your right."

Svanhild moved, then stopped.

"Yes, this looks good to me."

"And you think this tree will survive eleven hundred years and bring you back to us in the future?" Svanhild asked.

Holly looked at Einar. His gray eyes always made her feel steady. She loved that he was her rock, that he always had her back.

"Yes, Svanhild," Einar said. "Because you do not see a single tree around, it is unlikely that the tree was a coincidence. Holly said it was very, very old, thick, and tall. So it must have survived for hundreds of years."

"And it looks like I need to take matters into my hands." Holly smiled. "The Norn will only get me so far. Sometimes, your destiny is to make the decision to help yourself."

Svanhild's eyes rounded. "So you are sending a gift from the past to the future. To yourself?"

Holly nodded. "I guess I am."

Einar walked towards Svanhild. "Here, Holly?"

"Yes," she said.

While he began digging, she jumped slightly to let Baldr get higher on her hip. He was a big boy, dark blond as his father, his gray eyes always curious, always searching for something. He looked with fascination at Einar working, wriggled so that Holly would take him off her hip, and started toddling towards his father. He held on to Svanhild's skirt, and stood, watching.

"Papa," he said. "Papa."

Holly laughed. "He is probably thinking you're playing with dirt, just like he does with his toy shovel."

Holly took a small wooden bucket and a toy shovel that Einar had made for his son out of her travel bag, and Baldr stomped his feet with a squeal. He began digging, too, of course, awkwardly, not really helping. But Einar chuckled, and the whole family laughed.

"You little helper." Einar ruffled his son's hair.

Soon, the hole was deep enough, and Einar placed the seedling in it and put dirt over the roots, making sure it was planted securely. Holly felt like she wanted to say a blessing or something to protect the little ash tree that seemed so fragile and small against the strong wind, the vastness of the sea, and the endless, rolling hills behind it.

Einar hugged Holly closer, his arm around her shoulders. Loki arched his back and rubbed his ear against Svanhild's leg, then sat by her feet and hugged himself with his tail. Svanhild lifted Baldr into her arms, and the family looked at the ash tree.

"You spoke to me when I saw you in the Orkneys," Holly said to the tree. "There aren't many trees there, either, but something about you made me stop and look as I passed by. And then the idea came to me that I needed to plant a tree to allow the future me to travel back in time. And something within me knew that you were that tree."

She inhaled deeply and exhaled, trying to allow the emotions to pass through her and not make her tear up.

"You brought me to the man I love, to the man I am supposed to be with, to the man who makes me happy. The man who showed me that there's absolutely nothing wrong or faulty with me. The man who lets me bloom and live every day in gratitude for the happiness that he brought into my life. You brought me to the best daughter a woman could hope for—Svanhild. You brought me to have a child, and hopefully two more of my own, something I wished for since I was a little girl."

She squeezed Einar's hand that hugged her shoulder.

"I never met my biological parents, but I always wanted to be a biological mother to my children, to give them the feeling of the real support and love that a mother can give. I thought it was so important to be connected through blood, but now I see that family is about the love that ties us together. There is no difference between the love I have for Svanhild and the love I have for Baldr. I know now that my own parents truly love me and are my *real* parents, something my biological parents could never be. And who knew I'd need to cross eleven hundred years to realize it." She chuckled. "I guess you knew, little tree, didn't you?"

They all smiled, and Baldr shifted and held his little hands out to Holly. She took him from Svanhild and settled him on her hip.

"So, grow, tree of time. Grow strong, grow tall, grow to bring me here. Grow like my family is growing. Grow and set your roots deep here. And I will do the same with mine."

She hugged Einar and Svanhild and laid her cheek on her son's head. Her arms felt like long, broad branches, and she felt rooted, secure, and peaceful. Love spread through her whole being—the intense, passionate, soul-shattering love for Einar and the calm, warm, motherly love for her children.

And as she watched the wind rustling the young, pale-green leaves of the ash tree, she knew deep in her heart that this tree would survive and bring her home one day to Einar, where she was always supposed to be.

THANK you for reading VIKING'S DESIRE. I hope you loved Holly and Einar's story. Find out what happens next when the Norns send Cathy to meet her soulmate, Andor, in VIKING'S CLAIM.

SHE'S HIS ENEMY. But he can't stop fantasizing about her. When a sunny time traveler gets on the wrong side of a grumpy Viking, could his anger turn to passion?

READ VIKING'S CLAIM now >

☆☆☆☆☆ *"What a riveting read"*

SIGN-UP FOR MARIAH STONE'S Newsletter:

http://mariahstone.com/signup

FEELING LIKE A BILLION DOLLARS?

And the Norns are sending people to the future, too. If you

haven't read Channing and Ella's story yet, be sure to pick up AGE OF WOLVES.

There's more to tattooed billionaire, Channing Hakonson, than detective Ella O'Conner could have ever imagined—something mystical and ancient.

Read AGE OF WOLVES now >

⭐⭐⭐⭐⭐ *"Great twists and turns. I just couldn't stop reading!"*

Or stay in the Viking Age and read an excerpt from VIKING'S CLAIM.

Los Angeles, January 8, 2019

"That's better, Brad," Cathy said as she lifted the breathing tube to wipe the remaining shaving foam from her fiancé's chin. "I can see your face again."

She studied him, hoping for a twitch, a flutter of eyelashes, or any other sign. Nothing moved except for the pump of the ventilation machine next to him and the line of his heart monitor.

She forced a smile and said, "I believe in miracles. I believe you'll come back to me."

The affirmation felt increasingly fake the more times she said it, like she was lying to herself.

"You relax and rest, babe," she murmured. "When you get

out of this coma, you'll be groomed and fresh, as though you just slept for a long time." She kissed him on the tip of his nose.

Then she applied his favorite aftershave. She inhaled the masculine scent of it, her mind filling with memories of watching Brad in the bathroom mirror as he slapped it on his cheeks. He inevitably grimaced as it stung him, and he made that "ohh-ahhh" sound that always made her smile.

Cathy watched closely, hoping to see an echo of the grimace.

But none came.

She put the shaving accessories in her purse, then gently picked a dark-blond lock from his shoulder. "Yeah, babe, it's time for a haircut. Tomorrow."

The edges of his hair were bleached from the sunlight he had been exposed to every day being a professional surfer and instructor, but the new hair that had grown since he'd been in the ICU was the color of dark wheat. She wished she could look into his blue eyes again. She wished she could see him smile at her. Tell her how beautiful she looked today. Tell her how much he loved her.

Tears welled in Cathy's eyes. She cupped his jaw and brushed one of his high cheekbones with her thumb. "Come back to me, Brad," she whispered. "Please come back to me."

A knock made her jump and she stood up, quickly wiping her tears, then turned around. Dr. Gentzelman and Brad's dad, Eric, stood in the doorway. Eric was Brad's double, only older. Tall, well-built, with thick, blond hair that was already graying, he had the same blue eyes and a square jaw. But during the last twelve months, his shoulders had become slouched and dark circles had appeared under his eyes. And for the first time, Cathy noticed that he had begun to look like an old man.

"Hi, Cathy," Dr. Gentzelman said. "Are we interrupting?"

Cathy pressed out a smile. “No, no. Of course not. Sorry, I’m just a bit emotional today.”

Dr. Gentzelman shook her head and smiled back politely. “Don’t apologize. I can’t imagine how hard it must be for you.” She looked at Eric and added. “For both of you.”

The lines around Eric’s mouth deepened.

Cathy tucked her hair behind her ear. “I was already leaving, so you can have your time with him.”

She took her purse and was about to walk out when Eric said, “I need to talk to you, Cathy.”

With a sinking feeling in her stomach, Cathy gave a curt nod and looked at him.

“He isn’t getting better,” he said. “It’s been more than a year. Linda and I—we want to let him go.”

Cathy closed her eyes, pain crushing, whirling, knocking her, stealing the ground under her feet.

When she opened her eyes, Dr. Gentzelman and Eric were all blurry. “No,” Cathy said.

“You need to consider it, Cathy,” Dr. Gentzelman said. “I’m so sorry to say this, but Brad’s coma is most likely permanent. His brain shows almost no signs of activity, and after a year, the chances of him returning are almost null. We are keeping his body breathing and supplying it with nutrients, but Brad is not with us anymore.”

Cathy shook her head. “You don’t know that. He could still be in there. People come out of comas all the time.”

“Not after a year, Cathy.”

Eric’s chin trembled. He was looking at the floor, but finally he raised his eyes, red and watery. “You’re torturing him, Cathy. You’re torturing us—all of us, yourself included. He wants to go. Let him!”

He might as well have punched her in the stomach. She stopped breathing from the pain she heard in his words.

Seeing her reaction, Eric pressed. "He should never have given you the power to decide this. We're his parents. If the legal decision was in our hands, we'd already have let him go. We're ready."

Dr. Gentzelman covered Cathy's hand with hers. "Maybe it's time you get ready, too."

Tears fell down Cathy's face. Her chest hurt. Hell, her whole body hurt. "No! While there's still hope—"

"But there isn't!" Eric yelled.

Dr. Gentzelman shook her head. "I'm so sorry."

Cathy looked back at Brad, who was lying peacefully, as though he was just asleep and would wake up and they'd go to the beach. "I do *not* accept that," she said. "If I'm the only one fighting for his life, well then so be it."

Eric sighed and pinched the bridge of his nose. "We'll give you two weeks to come to terms with letting him go, Cathy. If you don't give your permission in two weeks, we'll take legal action. I can't allow you to keep my son trapped here in this bed when I know he wants to go."

Hot waves of anger and fear hit Cathy in the face. She whirled around, bent down and kissed Brad's cheek. The after-shave mixed with his scent filled her nostrils. She stopped for a moment before Eric. "Please, hear me. I do *not* give my permission to stop his life support. Do you understand?" She turned to Dr. Gentzelman. "You are not allowed to stop those machines."

Cathy waited for Dr. Gentzelman's small nod then stormed out of the hospital room.

She made her way out of the building on autopilot, Eric's words thundering in her ears, until she came to a stop at her yellow Volkswagen New Beetle in the parking lot. Getting inside made her feel like a giant trying to fit into a porcelain cup. She would so much rather drive a Range Rover, which would fit her height and size much better. But Brad was right. Small cars saved the environment and made parking easier, and the color radiated the sun.

Radiated California.

So unlike her.

But as long as their surfboards fit, that was all they needed.

Cathy had already strapped her board to the roof rack as she'd planned on catching some waves after teaching her yoga class. But after the conversation she'd just had, yoga was the last thing on her mind. She called in sick with the studio then maneuvered out of the hospital parking lot into the surprisingly warm winter's day.

Anger and desperation whirled inside her, boiling, bashing.

She needed to be at the beach. Where everything had started. Where she'd first met Brad five years ago. Where they had planned to open a surf and yoga school. Where they were supposed to get married.

And where the people who were supposed to be his friends had driven Brad away—to his death.

*Not death!* He was not dead yet.

The drive to Sonada Beach crawled, and Cathy watched the familiar scene flash by—the houses, palm trees and hills she had seen countless times on the same ride with Brad. Finally, Cathy parked up the hill and quickly changed into her wetsuit. It was hot pink—Brad had chosen the color as a joke.

"This will scream 'California girl,'" he'd said through his laughter when she'd opened the gift and her jaw had hit the floor.

The truth was, Cathy couldn't feel any less like a California girl in it. Despite being vegan for eight years, despite hours of daily yoga, her body just wanted to stay curvy. Underneath the fat were muscles, but in the wetsuit Cathy felt like a giant hot-pink ball of human flesh.

She missed him physically, as though she were a bird and her wings no longer worked without him. Maybe being in the ocean would help her connect with him. Find his spirit, ask it to go back to him. Maybe he was just lost somewhere out there, in the waves, and if she found him, she could help him return to his body.

Or maybe that was just a bunch of New Age crap.

Cathy gathered her hair into a messy bun, took her surfboard and walked down a rocky path towards the white beach hidden between the hills.

She spotted them from above. Cathy was willing to sell her soul to the Devil for a chance that they wouldn't notice her. But even the Devil couldn't hide her glowing hot-pink wetsuit. The five of them stopped before Cathy, four middle-aged men and Miranda. The guys were not in the best form, a couple of them with beer bellies. Jason was the most chiseled. Miranda was petite but had the physique of a bodybuilder and the tan of someone who spent hours in the sun. They scowled at her.

"What are you doing here?" Miranda said. "You're not allowed on the beach."

Cathy curled into a ball internally. Most surfers weren't like these guys. Most were like Brad, laid-back, traveling the world and enjoying the ocean. Miranda and the gang never left California. They'd grown up with one of the most magnificent beaches in the world right in their backyard, and they refused to share it. Unfortunately, surf localists weren't just a problem here. And the police couldn't do anything about them, nor could public protests.

But she wouldn't let them get to her this time. "Are you continuing your bullying, even after what happened to Brad? Seriously, you guys are like teenagers on a schoolyard. Grow up."

"Maybe so," Jason said. "But someone needs to protect our

beach. Look at this." He swept a hand towards the beach. There were just three people in the water and no one except Cathy and the group on the beach. The bay was spectacular. Smooth sand, tall cliffs, and waves breaking against a point. "Why do you think Sonada isn't crowded like Malibu or El Porto? Because we protect it. Brad grew up here, too. He became a world champion being trained on these waves, in this freedom. If we allow every tourist here, you wouldn't be able to spit without hitting someone."

"Especially if you guys had opened your damn yoga and surfing school," Miranda said.

Yes, that was the reason they had driven him away from the beach, making him choose, Cathy or the group. Cathy or the beach.

He'd chosen Cathy.

*Fight for yourself, Cathy. Stand up to them like he did.*

"You guys aren't even sorry," she said. "Don't you see that he almost died because of you?"

Miranda shook her head. Jason looked down, his nostrils flaring.

"If you want to blame anyone for what happened to him," Miranda said. "Blame yourself. He was one of us. Our world champion. He'd never have left the beach if it wasn't for you. You planted the idea of opening that school in his head."

Cathy's throat clenched.

"Stop it, Miranda," Jason said. "There won't be a school anymore. Not without Brad."

Cathy's eyes blurred, her chest tightened. He was right. Not without Brad.

Jason looked at Cathy, and his face softened. "Just for him, stay and surf. Only today, though. Don't come back. It's hard for all of us."

He tugged Miranda after him, and the five of them walked away.

Were they seriously blaming her for Brad's accident? Worse, were they right? Her stomach twisted with doubt. If he hadn't chosen her, he'd likely still be well and whole, living his life.

On shaky legs, her arms like cooked noodles, she walked to the ocean. The crash of the waves familiar and soothing, Cathy walked into the cool water, her feet numbing from the cold. She set the board on the water, jumping over waves, then lay on it and began paddling into the open sea. The wind wasn't strong today and the waves weren't the best for surfing. But she didn't really want to surf anyway. She just wanted to be out on the water.

To connect with Brad.

With the beach far behind her, she stopped paddling and sat on the board, legs hanging from either side.

Maybe Brad's soul was somewhere around here. Maybe it was deep down at the bottom of the sea where he'd hit his head. Maybe Cathy should dive and see if she could find it.

Or maybe she should just dive and stay down. Period.

Maybe she and Brad would be together again.

She looked down into the dark blue water. Maybe she should just let go.

Someone splashed cold water in her face. Cathy gasped, her eyes burning from the salt. She looked up and through stinging lids, saw an old lady on a board.

Cathy was so astounded she almost fell off when a wave rocked her.

"Hello, dear," the lady said.

She was dressed in a black wetsuit with salad-green stripes. Her white hair was gathered in a small bun at her neck, and her eyes were the most peculiar color—well, they were changing color, it seemed. Or maybe they were all colors at the same time.

"H-hello," Cathy said.

The woman lifted her face to the sun. "Lovely day, isn't it?"

Cathy looked around, just to make sure the lady was talking to her. "Yes. It is. I'm sorry, are you okay? Do you need any help getting back to shore?"

"Oh no, dear. I'm wonderful. It is you who needs help."

Cathy looked down at the board. Maybe it was damaged and she hadn't noticed? But it looked perfectly fine.

"What are you talking about?"

"Dying here is not your destiny."

Cathy considered herself a spiritual person. She felt there was a higher power in the universe and believed in the law of attraction. She taught yoga.

But she had never experienced the feeling she was having now. It was as if cold sparks of electricity crawled under her skin. "How do you know?" she asked.

"You won't find his soul down there, dear. And even if you did, that wouldn't bring him back."

A painful knot formed in Cathy's throat, and she forced herself to inhale deeply and slowly, then counted to four, then breathed out again counting to four. She might be crazy, but there was something about this woman.

"Can you help me get him back?" Cathy said.

"Oh, but sweetheart, you can't help him. However, there is a man you *can* help. The man who is destined for you."

Cathy frowned. "Do you mean Brad?"

The woman smiled as if Cathy was a cute but silly child. "It's not Brad, although Brad is partly him." She shook her head. "Less talk, more action."

She unzipped a key pocket on her thigh and produced a

strangely large object for the size of the pocket. How had she gotten it in there?

The object glistened in her hands like gold. Well, it was gold.

A spindle.

Its smooth surface was covered with beautiful engravings that Cathy recognized from the Norse mythology that had always interested her.

She looked into the serene wrinkled face of the woman. "Who are you?"

"I am exactly what you are afraid to believe I am. Now, sweetheart, we do not have much time. There is a man who needs you to save him. In return, he will save you."

The woman held out the spindle to Cathy, and, bewildered, Cathy watched it.

"Hurry," the woman pressed. "The battle is about to begin, and then it'll be too late."

All this sounded too strange even for Cathy, but she couldn't stop staring at the spindle. Her hand reached out of its own accord. When she touched the spindle, a soft meditative state enveloped her.

The world around her began disappearing—the sky, the coast, the lady. All that was left was the surf splashing and the lady's voice, "You are going to travel back in time."

And then, as if it was a wave lifting her up and throwing her down, Cathy plunged into it. The energy washed through her and carried her toward an unknown shore.

And then everything went dark...

**KEEP READING NOW VIKING'S CLAIM.**

# Also by Mariah Stone

## Mariah's Time Travel Romance Series

- Called by a Highlander
- Called by a Viking
- Called by a Pirate
- Fated

## Mariah's Regency Romance Series

- Dukes and Secrets

## View All of Mariah's Books in Reading Order

Scan the QR code for the complete list of Mariah's ebooks, paperbacks, and audiobooks in reading order.

# ENJOY THE BOOK? YOU CAN MAKE A DIFFERENCE!

Please, leave your honest review for the book.

As much as I'd love to, I don't have financial capacity like New York publishers to run ads in the newspaper or put posters in subway.

But I have something much, much more powerful!

**Committed and loyal readers.**

If you enjoyed the book, I'd be so grateful if you could spend five minutes leaving a review on the book's **sales page.**

Thank you very much!

# GET A FREE MARIAH STONE BOOK!

Join Mariah's mailing list to be the first to know of new releases, free books, special prices, and other author giveaways.

freehistoricalromancebooks.com

# NOTE ON HISTORICAL ACCURACY

A real historical figure inspired me to write Einar.

One of the first jarls of the Orkneys, Torf-Einarr, freed the Orkneys from the outlaws and chased and killed Thorir Tree-beard among other pirates in the late ninth century. Besides that, the real Torf-Einarr was the only son who avenged the murder of his father, Jarl Rögnvald, even though his father hadn't treated Einarr well because he was born to a slave.

Einarr also negotiated the ownership of the Orkneys with the king and established a Norse dynasty that ruled the islands until the fifteenth century.

I loved his story: an underdog stepping in and rising to heights most men back then only dreamed of.

And while my Einar has a different story and is dealing with different issues, I hope my fascination with the man that inspired the character comes through and lets him shine.

Thank you for reading this story, and I hope you enjoyed Einar as much as I enjoyed researching and writing him!

Yours,

Mariah Stone

# ACKNOWLEDGMENTS

This is my favorite part of writing the book. THANK YOU:

Laura Barth, my amazing editor, without whom I cannot imagine writing another book.

My husband and my son, the two most important people in my world.

My parents thanks to whom I am where I am.

My loyal, wonderful readers, who make it possible for me to see my family every day instead of working as a business consultant and living in hotels.

My local writer group whom I see every two weeks and who always give me a nudge to be better and to go on.

# About Mariah Stone

Mariah Stone is a bestselling author of time travel romance novels, including her popular Called by a Highlander series and her hot Viking, Pirate, and Regency novels. With nearly one million books sold, Mariah writes about strong modern-day women falling in love with their soulmates across time. Her books are available worldwide in multiple languages in e-book, print, and audio.

Subscribe to Mariah's newsletter for a free time travel book today at mariahstone.com/signup!

facebook.com/mariahstoneauthor
instagram.com/mariahstoneauthor
bookbub.com/authors/mariah-stone
pinterest.com/mariahstoneauthor
amazon.com/Mariah-Stone/e/B07JVW28PJ